Cindy Radler

THE HAPPY HOLLISTERS
AND THE SECRET
OF THE LUCKY COINS

The Happy Hollisters and the Secret of the Lucky Coins

BY JERRY WEST

Illustrated by Helen S. Hamilton

GARDEN CITY, N.Y.

Doubleday & Company, Inc.

Contents

CHAPTER 1

A SURPRISE PENNY

"RICKY! Holly! I have a secret!" cried Sue Hollister. Holding one chubby fist behind her back, she ran along the sidewalk toward her brother and sister.

Holly, six, was two years older than Sue. Her hair was braided in pigtails, which usually were flying straight out. At the moment Holly was walking slowly, eating a vanilla ice cream cone.

Ricky was seven. He had freckles, red hair and an impish grin. The strawberry cone he was eating was halfway gone. "Hi, Sue!" he said, when they came face to face. "What's your big secret?"

"I can't show anybody until I get home. The lady said not to."

"What lady?" Ricky asked impatiently.

"The parakeet lady, that's who."

Holly's tongue flicked out to catch a drip of ice cream. "Do you mean a lady parakeet?" she asked.

"Oh no," replied Sue, shaking her head so that her black bobbed hair swished from side to side. "This lady wasn't a bird. She *had* a bird."

Quickly the little girl explained that a pet parakeet had flown out of an open window. The woman who owned it was trying to coax the bird back into its cage when Sue came along.

"The parakeet was sitting on a hedge," Sue declared, "and I caught it in my hands."

"Yikes! That was keen!" Ricky said, proudly. "But what's that got to do with your secret?"

Sue explained that she had carried the parakeet into the lady's house and placed it in its cage. "Then I got a reward! That's the secret."

"Oh, I know what it is," Ricky said. "You're holding a nickel behind your back."

Sue giggled and replied, "No, it's littler than that."

"A penny?" Holly said.

When Sue had nodded vigorously, Ricky nibbled at the edge of his disappearing cone and said, "What's so secret about a penny?"

"It's a lucky penny," Sue replied. "But I'm not going to show it to you!"

"I'll give you two licks of my ice cream cone if you will," Holly offered.

Sue accepted and took one lick. Then she held out her fist and opened it. In the palm of her hand was a copper coin much larger than the pennies the children were used to seeing. Around the edge were thirteen stars. In the center was a Liberty head and beneath it the date 1817.

Ricky looked at the coin solemnly, as if he knew all about 1817 pennies. "What's lucky about that big jumbo?" he asked, popping the last bit of cone into his mouth.

"Daddy will know," Sue retorted and bent forward to take another lick from Holly's ice cream.

"Ow!" Holly complained. "You're taking a bite, not a lick!" She pulled the cone back, but the ice cream tilted out and dropped to the sidewalk.

Plop!

"Oh!" Sue exclaimed. "I'm sorry! Here take my penny."

"No, thanks," Holly said, "I think your penny's unlucky."

Just then a beautiful collie dog ran out of the Hollisters' driveway halfway down the block. "Here Zip!" Holly called. The girl pointed to the spilled ice cream and the collie lapped it up eagerly.

"I'm glad it wasn't wasted," Holly declared as the three children, with Zip bounding at their heels, ran onto their front lawn.

The Hollisters' home, located in the town of Shoreham, was a large, rambling house. The big lawn in front extended around both sides, and the rear of the property bordered beautiful Pine Lake where a rowboat rocked at its mooring off the dock.

Halfway between there and the back of the house was a circular flower bed. Kneeling beside it were Mrs. Hollister and her two other children, Pete and Pam. They were helping their mother transplant marigolds to edge the garden.

Mrs. Hollister, a pretty slender woman with light hair, stood up and pulled off her garden gloves. "Thanks for helping me, Pete and Pam," she said, smiling.

"It was fun," Pete replied. He was twelve years old and had blond crew-cut hair and a happy smile.

His sister Pam, ten, wore her golden hair in a fluffy bob. She gave the freshly turned earth a few extra pats, then stood up as Ricky, Holly, and Sue raced into the back yard.

When the story of the lucky penny was told, Mrs. Hollister said, "Your daddy will probably know why it's lucky. Here he comes now!"

The children turned to see a station wagon pull into the driveway. When it stopped, Mr. Hollister stepped out. He was a tall, handsome, athletic-looking man, who walked toward them with an easy stride. Mr. Hollister owned The Trading Post, a combination toy, hardware, and sporting goods shop in the center of Shoreham.

When Sue raced over to her father, he picked her up and somersaulted her onto his shoulders. Then with giggles and laughs, the children trooped into the house and hastily washed their hands and faces before sitting down to lunch.

Mr. Hollister was interested in the old coin and examined it carefully.

"Why is it lucky, Daddy?" Sue asked.

"Because it's probably worth more than a penny," Mr. Hollister replied. He explained that many old coins were scarce, and therefore collectors were willing to pay more for them than their original value.

"Well, we can find out about this one easily

enough, John," Mrs. Hollister said. "There's a coin shop not far from The Trading Post."

"That's right," her husband replied. "Mr. Steinberg is a numismatist. Fine chap, too!"

"A what?" Holly asked as she twisted one of her pigtails.

"A numismatist," Mr. Hollister replied. "That's a man who collects coins."

When lunch was over, Pete stood up eagerly. "Come on, let's go to the coin store now," he said.

All five children climbed into the station wagon and Mr. Hollister let them off in front of the coin shop. It was a tiny store squeezed between two other larger shops. A man, seated behind the counter, greeted them cheerfully.

"Mr. Steinberg," Pete began, "we're Mr. Hollister's children and we would like to ask a favor of you."

"Hmm, a couple of you resemble your dad," the man replied, smiling. "What can I do for you?"

Sue stepped up and handed him the old coin. "This is a lucky penny," the little girl announced. "Daddy thinks it's lucky because maybe it's worth more than a penny."

The man took the coin, looked at it on both sides, and said, "This is in good condition. It's worth two dollars."

"See!" Sue cried, looking up at Ricky and Holly, "it is a lucky coin, just like the parakeet lady said."

"Crickets!" Pete declared. "If old coins are worth

"It's worth two dollars."

that much money, perhaps it would be a good idea to start collecting them."

"It's a fine hobby," Mr. Steinberg said. "Why don't you begin by finding Lincoln pennies? It's lots of fun."

He showed the children a blue cardboard folder. Inside were rows of circular holes in which to place pennies. Under every cut-out was a printed date.

"The idea is to get a coin for each year," Mr. Steinberg explained.

"How much is the folder?" Holly asked.

"Twenty-five cents," the man replied.

"Okay," Pete said, "we'll buy it."

"I'll give you this catalogue telling about old Indian head pennies," Mr. Steinberg went on. "None of those have been made since 1909. You'll find all sorts of rare coins described in here."

After Pete had thanked him and paid for the penny folder, the man said, "What you should do first is go to the bank and buy a dollar's worth of pennies. In that way you'll find many Lincoln heads to put into your collection."

The children thanked him again and left the store, heading directly for The Trading Post.

"That's a great idea Mr. Steinberg had," Pete said, grinning, "except that we don't have a dollar."

"We could earn it," Pam suggested.

"Where can we get a job?" Holly asked.

"At The Trading Post!" Ricky said. "Maybe Dad will hire us." Even Sue thought this would be a good

15

idea. She gave her lucky coin to Pete for safekeeping and he put it into his pocket.

When they entered their father's store, Mr. Hollister had just finished waiting on a customer.

This time Sue did not race up to greet him. Instead, she said, "Mr. Hollister, we're looking for jobs."

"Yes!" Ricky put in with a mischievous grin. "We have to earn a dollar." Quickly they told about their visit to Mr. Steinberg's shop and showed their father the coin folder.

"Good! I'm glad you've found a new hobby," Mr. Hollister said. "I do have a job for you. Come with me."

He led them to the back of the store, then out a side door which led to an alley. There stood a carton nearly as tall as Pete. It had been opened at the top and was full of smaller boxes with the name *Snake Charmer* printed on the top of each.

"Here's your job," Mr. Hollister said. "Carry these carefully into the shop and put them on the toy shelf. When you've finished I'll give you a dollar."

"Yikes!" Ricky said. "What's a Snake Charmer, Dad?"

"It's a new toy," his father replied. "When you have finished your job, I'll let you see one. But don't open them until then."

"Oh goody! Another surprise!" Sue remarked happily.

Pete reached into the carton and removed the

small boxes carefully, giving each of the other children two or three at a time to carry inside. He was nearly finished with the chore when two boys walked into the alley. Ricky saw them first.

"Pst! Look who's coming, Pete!"

His brother glanced up to see Joey Brill and Will Wilson approaching. Joey was Pete's age but heavier. He usually looked unpleasant and was continually making trouble for the Hollisters. His friend Will was about the same size and trailed around after Joey, whom he liked for some reason unknown to the Hollisters.

Without saying hello, Joey started to laugh at Pete. "Ha-ha, your father's making you work!" he taunted.

Pete did not reply, but Holly, stepping out of the door, heard the remark and said, "We're earning some money, that's what!"

"Ha!" Will chimed in. "You must be pretty poor to have to work."

"It's none of your business," Pete told him. "Now go away."

Joey leaned over to glance into the large carton, which was now nearly empty. He saw the small boxes. "Snake Charmer," he said. "What's that? Something new?"

"It's a toy of some kind," Pam replied as Pete handed her several boxes.

"You mean you don't know?" Joey asked with a look of mock surprise. "Here, let's open one."

17

"Don't touch it!" Pete said, pushing Joey's hand away. "We're not to look until we finish this job."

"You mean you let your father boss you around?" Joey sneered.

"Get out of here!" Pete ordered. "This is private property."

"All right," the bully retorted. He turned as if to leave, but suddenly thrust his hand into the carton and pulled out a Snake Charmer box.

"Put that down," Pete said. He tried to grab the box, but missed as Joey and Will raced out of the alley and into the street.

Instantly Pete and Pam gave chase. The two boys, however, managed to cross the street on a green light. It turned red as Pete and his sister stepped off the curb.

"Just our luck!" Pete said as he waited for traffic to pass by. The children crossed the street into the small park which was located in the center of town. They looked up and down but Joey and Will were nowhere to be seen.

"How could they have vanished?" Pam wondered.

"Oh look!" Pete said, pointing to the far side of the green. "The bushes behind the park bench moved. Maybe they're hiding there."

Darting from one tree to another, Pete and Pam concealed themselves until they were quite close to the heavy cement park bench. They could see Joey and Will hiding behind it.

Pete heard Will whisper hoarsely, "Okay, there's no sign of them. Let's open the box now."

Before Pete and Pam could spring upon the pair, Joey twisted the lid of the box. The next second he let out a wild shriek!

CHAPTER 2

A FUNNY TRICK

A BIG fat snake made of cloth and wire popped out of the box and flew through the air between Will and Joey. Before the bullies could recover from their fright, Pete and Pam leaped from their hiding place. The girl grabbed the snake while her brother retrieved the box.

"Wh—why didn't you tell us that was a scary toy?" red-faced Joey asked angrily.

"I told you we didn't know what was in the box," Pete replied.

"It serves you right," Pam said as she squeezed the snake back into its container. "Next time, don't try to steal anything from our father's store!"

"Aw, we were only borrowing it for a minute," said Will.

But Joey had not finished with his trickery. He snatched for the toy again. As he did, Pete grappled with him. They rolled over and over on the grass. Being heavier, Joey sat on top of Pete, but the Hollister boy arched his back and the bully flew off, landing hard. Pete scrambled to his feet as his opponent picked himself up slowly off the grass.

"You don't have to get so rough," Joey complained. "Come on, Will, these Hollisters can't take a joke."

The two bullies hurried across the street while Pete and Pam returned to The Trading Post. By the time they arrived, Ricky, Holly, and Sue had carried the remaining boxes into the store.

"Did you catch those rascals?" Mr. Hollister asked.

"Yes, and here's the Snake Charmer," Pam said.

"It looks a little shopworn," their father remarked. Then he opened the cash register and gave a dollar to Pam. "Here's your pay. You may keep the Snake Charmer as a bonus."

"Thanks, Dad," the children chorused.

Each took a turn making the fat cloth snake jump high into the air. Then, with Holly carrying the new toy, they went to the red brick bank building at the end of the street.

Tellers' windows ran along both sides of the marble interior. At the far end, the huge, round door of a safe deposit vault stood open. Ricky was fascinated by the barred inner door and the rows of shiny boxes inside.

While Pam and the others made their way to a teller, Ricky walked to the back of the bank where a man was about to enter the low gate in front of the vault. An attendant seated behind the barricade pressed a buzzer, and the gate opened. The man stepped through it, and Ricky walked in behind him. "Yikes, what a keen place for a hideout," Ricky thought as the attendant ushered the customer into the vault.

Ricky would have gone in too, had not Pam spied him. She hurried to the gate. "Ricky, come out of there at once," she whispered.

"Okay," her brother replied, but he lingered to gaze at the thick steel door.

"Come on, before they put us out of the bank!" Pam pleaded.

Ricky grinned and tried the knob on the gate. It would not turn. "I guess I have to press the buzzer," he said, and glanced at the table where the guard had been seated. He saw two buttons on the side of it, one white, the other black. Ricky pushed the black button, but it did not move. He tugged and it came out a little, but nothing happened.

"Try the other one," Pam suggested.

When the boy stabbed it with his finger, the buzzer sounded and Pam held the gate open.

"You imp," she said, smiling. "Now stay with me until I get the pennies."

With her brothers and sisters looking on, Pam presented their dollar to the teller. "We'd like a hundred pennies," she said.

The teller looked down and saw the coin album in her hand. "Is this a new hobby?" he asked.

"Yes, it is," the girl replied. "We just started today."

"Coins have become a very popular hobby," the teller said. "Our customers are always asking for pennies, nickels, dimes, and even silver dollars." He slid two rolls of fifty pennies across the counter.

"Thank you," Pam said and hesitated a moment. "Would you like to see a real ancient penny?"

"Yes, of course. Do you have one with you?"

Pete reached into his pocket to get the 1817 penny. Suddenly a look of dismay came over his face. He pulled out a penknife, a button, a large nail, a dime and a whistle, but no penny.

"Oh!" said Pam. "You must have lost it while you were wrestling with Joey!"

"Let's go back and find it right away," Pete said.

When the children started toward the front door, two policemen suddenly swept inside, with drawn revolvers.

"Nobody move!" one of them commanded.

"Oh!" Holly said in alarm, and clung to Pete's arm.

A woman standing at another window screamed as five more policemen swarmed in through back and side doors. One of them was Officer Cal Newberry, the handsome young man who was a special friend of the Hollisters.

Sue ran over to him and threw her arms around one of his legs. "Hello!" she cried brightly. "Is this a game you're playing?"

Without a word, Cal pushed the little girl gently aside and joined his mates in a thorough search of the bank. After a few tense moments, everybody started talking at once.

"Quiet, please," ordered one of the officers, whom Pete recognized as Captain Walters. "Who set off the alarm?"

Nobody said anything, but Pam's face grew suddenly red and her eyes darted to the buttons on the table behind the gate. She shot a glance at Ricky, who rolled his eyes in despair.

"Somebody must have pulled the alarm," the captain repeated sternly. "How about you, Mr. Clark?" he asked the vault attendant.

Pam bent over Ricky's shoulder. "You'd better tell them quickly," she whispered.

Ricky gulped twice. The cowlick on his red hair stood straighter than ever. He tried to speak, but no words came out. Pam nudged him.

Then Ricky cleared his throat and said in a tiny voice, "I guess I did."

"What was that? Speak up, young man," the captain ordered.

Officer Cal stepped quickly to Ricky's side and put his arm around his shoulder. "Tell us about it," he said kindly.

Ricky's eyes brimmed with tears, and his chin quivered. "I—I pulled the black button," he said, "but I didn't know it was for the police, honest!"

"Phew!" said the captain, and holstered his gun. "Well boys, that was quick work. We got here in three minutes flat after the alarm sounded at headquarters." He turned to Ricky. "Don't pull a trick

24

like that again, sonny. You've already scared these bank people out of a year's growth."

"Me, too," Ricky replied shakily. "I won't grow any more till I'm eight."

The policemen left, and the Hollisters hurried out of the bank as quickly as they could.

"Yikes, that was just like on television," Ricky said when they reached the street.

But even their adventure had not made them forget about the missing coin. They walked swiftly to the park bench, where Pete had tussled on the grass with Joey. After ten minutes of searching, they all had green grass stains on their knees, but no old coin!

"Maybe Joey or Will picked it up," Holly ventured. "There they are now." She pointed across the street where the two boys were entering the candy store.

"Maybe they're going to spend our penny!" Ricky said hotly.

"I'll find out!" Pete declared. Taking Sue by the hand, he crossed the street. The others followed. They met Joey and Will coming out of the store, stripping wrappers from sticks of chewing gum.

"Did you buy that with the penny you found?" Pete asked.

"No, I had a nickel," Will said. "Hey, what's this about a penny?"

"We lost an old penny worth two dollars," Ricky spoke up. "We thought maybe you found it."

"How can a penny be worth two dollars?" Joey scoffed.

"Well, our penny was!" declared Sue.

"Phooey!" Will said rudely, and waved three sticks of chewing gum under Pete's nose. "I'm going to give these to my *friends*," he said as the pair laughed and sauntered away.

Disappointed, the Hollisters started home. It was a long walk, and Sue had trouble keeping up with the others. When her chubby little legs grew tired, Pete and Pam took turns giving her a pickaback ride.

At last they hurried into their driveway, where Zip barked a welcome and bounded around them.

Holly scampered eagerly toward the dock, where she had set out her fishing line earlier that morning.

"I'll bet I've caught a catfish!" she called back.

Pete, Pam, Ricky and Sue hurried into the house. "Mommy!" Sue cried, skipping into the living room. "We've got pennies and a Sna—"

"Hush!" Pam whispered. "Don't tell Mother about the Snake Charmer yet. Maybe we can fool her." Pam held the toy behind her back.

"Hello, my dears," Mrs. Hollister said as she removed her apron and stepped from the kitchen to greet them. "Did you have any luck in town?"

Pete grinned. "Some good and some bad." Silence followed as the children eyed each other. Then Ricky blurted out his story and Sue giggled.

Mrs. Hollister looked at Ricky sternly, shook her head and sighed.

26

"Guess what, Mother," Pete said quickly to change the subject. "We have a new hobby—coin collecting."

He showed his mother the blue album and the two rolls of fifty pennies. Quickly he tore off the maroon wrappers and spilled the pennies on the rug. Everyone, even Mrs. Hollister, sat down cross-legged, examining the dates on the coins.

"This is going to be real fun," their mother said gaily. "People have been collecting coins for hundreds of years."

"What did they use for money before coins were invented?" Ricky asked.

As Pam busily placed pennies of various dates into the holes of the album, Mrs. Hollister explained that primitive people used sea shells and animal teeth to buy the things they wanted.

"Ugh!" exclaimed Pete. "Imagine carrying around a pocketful of teeth!"

Mrs. Hollister added that the early American settlers had used beaver skins, shell beads called *wampum*, and even tobacco in exchange for goods.

"Crickets, Mother, you're smart!" Pete said as he gathered all the duplicate coins into one pile. "We now have ten pennies in our collection. What'll we do with the rest of these?"

"Let's divide them," Pam replied, "and drop them into our piggy banks."

As Pam counted out five piles of pennies, Pete said, "Mother, we didn't tell you about the unlucky thing that happened today. I lost Sue's lucky penny!"

"Oh dear!" Mrs. Hollister cried. "That's too bad." Pete told her about what had occurred. "Did you look everywhere?"

"I think so."

"There's one favorite place for coins to hide," Mrs. Hollister went on, smiling. "Did you look in the cuffs of your trousers?"

"Crickets, no!" Pete said. His fingers quickly searched in the cuff of his left leg. Nothing there. Then he ran his index finger around the other cuff. His eyes opened wide with amazement. He pulled out the missing penny!

"Hurray!" Ricky shouted.

Sue jumped up and flung her arms around her mother's neck. "I love you, Mommy!" she said, "for finding my lucky coin."

"What a surprise!" Pam declared happily.

Sue leaned over and whispered to her, "May we show Mother the other surprise now?"

Her sister nodded, took the Snake Charmer from behind her back and thrust it into her mother's hands.

"Open the lid," the girl said, her eyes twinkling.

Mrs. Hollister tilted the box forward, opened the top and *zingg!*—the snake flew out and hit Pam on the nose!

"Ow!" she exclaimed, and then laughed. "Mother, you fooled me!"

Everyone giggled at the joke that had backfired,

Zingg! The snake hit Pam on the nose.

and Mrs. Hollister laughed so hard that tears came to her eyes. When she had wiped them away with her handkerchief, she said, "This certainly is a day full of surprises, and I have another big one to tell you!"

CHAPTER 3

A MYSTERIOUS NOISE

"ANOTHER surprise!" Pam cried. "Oh please tell us what it is," she begged.

"I received a telephone call from Aunt Marge," Mrs. Hollister said, "and she would like us to spend a few days with them in Crestwood."

"That's great!" Pete cried, and punched a sofa cushion with glee. "It'll be neat to see our old town again."

The Hollisters had lived in Crestwood before they moved to Shoreham. Mr. Hollister's brother Russ, his wife Marge and their two children, Teddy and Jean, still lived there.

Uncle Russ, who drew a daily cartoon strip for a number of newspapers, was the Hollister children's favorite uncle, and they always had a good time with their cousins Teddy and Jean.

"Oh goody!" Sue said, clapping her hands. "Maybe Aunt Marge will make us some of her extra special cookies."

"Well if you children approve," their mother said with a laugh, "Daddy and I would like to make the trip. He needs a rest from The Trading Post."

"Yes, Daddy's been working very hard," Ricky

said seriously. "I think we should all give him a vacation."

"Then we'll return Aunt Marge's phone call to-
night after supper," Mrs. Hollister said, and Ricky
did a double-flip somersault on the rug.

"Yikes! Let's tell Holly!" he exclaimed and jumped
to his feet.

"Would you like some hot gingerbread and milk,
first?" Mrs. Hollister asked, smiling. "You can take
Holly's out to her when you're finished."

There was a rousing chorus of "yes!" and the children trooped after their mother into the kitchen. As
she served them each a dark, spicy square of cake,
they talked excitedly about the coming trip.

Outside Holly barely heard their happy voices as
she knelt on the end of the dock and waited patiently
for a fish to bite on her line. The string dipped. She
gave it a tug. Something tugged back!

"Ooh, I've got one!" Holly said, and started to
pull in the black line. A few feet away there was a
big splash in the water as the hooked fish jumped
into the air. Quickly Holly pulled it to the dock. "It's
a whopping sunfish," she said to herself. With the
end of her tongue peeping out between her lips, the
girl tried to take the wriggling fish off the hook.

She had nearly worked it loose when a canoe came
into sight around the bend in the shore line. Holly
glanced up to see Joey and Will paddling quickly
toward the dock. When they reached it, Joey glided
alongside. "I've got news for you," he told Holly.

"Yeah," Will said. "We found the coin you lost."

"You did?" Holly asked, holding her line with the fish still on it. "Oh thanks. Now Pete won't feel so bad."

"But we want a reward for finding it," Joey declared.

"I'll give you my fish," Holly offered.

"Okay, but first you'll have to identify the coin," Joey said. "This might be the wrong one."

Holly leaned forward toward Joey's clenched fist. As she did, the boy grabbed her arm and tried to pull her into the water.

"Ow, let go!" Holly cried. Her shout was heard by Zip, and he came on the run, barking loudly. Fearing that the big collie might jump right into his canoe, Joey let go of Holly. But he had thrown her off balance. As she teetered on the dock, her arms flapping, the sunfish flew off the hook.

Splat! The fish hit Joey in the face. The startled boy fell backward and landed in the bottom of the canoe with the fish flopping beside him. Will dipped his paddle deep into the water and the craft shot away from the dock.

Having heard the commotion, the other children ran out of the house in time to see Joey throw the fish into the water. The bully shook his fist and vowed revenge on the Hollisters.

"What happened?" asked Pete, who was the first to reach the dock.

"Follow them!" Holly cried out. "They have the lucky coin!"

"No they haven't," Pete said, puzzled. "I have it right here in my pocket."

Holly looked confused until she heard what had happened in the house. When Pam told her of the proposed visit to Crestwood, Holly beamed. "Oh, we can have so much fun with Teddy and Jean!" she said. "And we'll get away from Joey for a while. He's an old meany!"

After supper that evening, Pam telephoned her cousins in Crestwood. Jean, who answered, was happy to hear that the Shoreham Hollisters had accepted the invitation.

"We have a new hobby here," Pam said, and told about their coin collection.

"That sounds like fun!" Jean replied. "You'll be visiting us at just the right time. There's an exhibit of rare coins being shown at the Crestwood Museum."

Jean said that the valuable collection had been bequeathed to the town by a wealthy local man named Eli Spencer. "People from all around are coming to see the exhibit," Jean said. "I know you'll enjoy it too."

The Hollisters spent the next day preparing for their trip. Pete talked with his chum, Dave Mead, who agreed to take care of Zip until the family returned. Mrs. Hollister suggested that Ann Hunter, Pam's friend, might care for White Nose, the cat, and her kittens. But in the flurry of packing no one remembered to call Ann.

The following morning everyone rose early, and the boys helped to carry the luggage to their station wagon.

"Say, what's going on here?" Mr. Hollister said jokingly as his sons lined up the suitcases beside the car. "Are we going on a year's vacation?"

"It looks that way," Pete said. "Can we get them all in the back, Dad?"

"I think we'll have to use the roof rack, Pete," came the reply. "It's in the garage. Will you fetch it?"

In a few minutes the boy returned with the rack, which he and his father attached firmly to the top of the station wagon. Half a dozen suitcases were lashed onto it and covered with a heavy tarpaulin.

"Now, that's secure," Mr. Hollister said as he gave the ropes a tug. "Is everybody ready?"

"We'll be there in a minute, John," Mrs. Hollister called from the house.

Just then Sue came down the front steps carrying a small carton in her arms. Part of an old lace curtain covered the top of the box, and was fastened down tightly with a piece of stout twine. Carefully Sue climbed up on the tail gate and shoved the carton onto the back seat. Then she sat down beside it. "I'm ready," she announced. "Come on, everybody."

After Mrs. Hollister had made a last minute check

to be sure that the windows were shut, she locked the house, Pete closed the garage doors and the family took their places in the car. Mr. and Mrs. Hollister sat in front; Pete, Pam and Ricky occupied the middle seat, while Holly and Sue sat in the back.

As if to say good-by to their home, Mr. Hollister honked twice as the car pulled out of the driveway. Soon they were out of town and on the road toward Crestwood. Mile after mile whizzed past beneath the humming wheels. They had been gone about an hour when Mrs. Hollister suddenly gasped. "Oh, poor White Nose and her kittens. We forgot about them!"

"Turn back, Daddy!" Holly cried. "They'll need milk and cat food."

Mr. Hollister did not want to do this. "We can telephone to Dave Mead when we get to the next town," he said.

"Yes," Pete agreed. "Dave knows where the key is hidden. He can get in and feed the cats."

Sue listened, and said nothing more than, "tsk, tsk." Mrs. Hollister thought that this was an unusual reaction for her youngest daughter, who loved White Nose and the kittens, but she said nothing.

Presently a sign at the side of the road informed motorists the next town was ten miles ahead. Halfway to it the children's father cocked his head and listened. "Do you hear that squeaking sound, Elaine?" he asked his wife.

Mrs. Hollister listened too. "Maybe your car needs greasing," she replied.

"It could be the springs," was Pete's guess. When he said this, Holly and Sue fell into each other's arms and giggled wildly.

"Yikes!" Ricky exclaimed. "What's so funny?"

"White Nose and her kittens are right here!" Sue declared proudly. "I didn't forget them, Mommy."

"Bless your heart!" Mrs. Hollister said, turning in her seat to look back at her daughters. Sue held up the box and pulled off the curtain covering. White Nose peeked over the edge, then cuddled down again with her kittens.

"I really didn't want to bring them with us," Mrs. Hollister remarked. "But since you have, you and Holly may take care of them."

"Oh yes, Mommy, we'll feed them," declared Sue. Kittens never were any trouble for her!

The family stopped for lunch, the kittens were fed, and once more the Hollisters went on their way. The afternoon was spent mainly playing with the baby cats, and the other children told Sue they were glad she brought the pets along.

As evening came on, Mr. Hollister said, "Look at those tourist cabins up ahead. Do you recognize them, children?"

"Yikes!" Ricky declared. "That's where we stayed when we moved to Shoreham."

"I recognize it," Pete declared.

"Me too," Pam said. She sounded less enthusi-

The mother cat peeked out.

astic. For it was where they had had their first experience with Joey Brill.

"Let's stay here overnight again," their father suggested. "It's just about halfway to Crestwood."

As soon as Mr. Hollister pulled into the circle of small cabins, the proprietor walked up to the car. "Hello," he said, and peered into the window. "Say!" he exclaimed. "You're the family who stayed with me some time ago on your way to Shoreham."

"That's right," Mr. Hollister replied, stepping out. "Now we're going back to visit Crestwood."

As the man showed them to their cabins, he said, "Come to think of it, this is quite a coincidence."

"How?" Pam asked.

"Remember that boy named Joey who released the brake on your car?"

"I'll say we do," Pete replied. "He lives in Shoreham."

"Well," the man said as he handed the keys to Mr. Hollister, "that same boy was here yesterday."

"Oh no!" Pam cried. "I hope he wasn't going to Crestwood!"

"No, I don't think so. His mother and father mentioned the town of Glenco," their host said as he left the family to unpack for the night.

"I've *heard* Joey talk about that place," Pete said. "He has relatives who live there."

Next morning as the Hollisters set off again, they heard the news broadcast over their car radio. A stormy day was predicted, and the skies already were lead gray with low clouds swept along by a stiff breeze. The announcer concluded with a special warning. "Tornados are expected in the area," he said, "and motorists are advised to exercise caution."

"Oh, John," Mrs. Hollister said, "I hope we don't get caught in a twister!"

But by mid-morning the wind had increased greatly. The children could feel it buffet the car as they sped along the highway. Then suddenly they heard a flapping, snapping noise.

"Crickets!" Pete declared. "The tarpaulin's loose on the roof, Dad."

Suddenly the noise stopped and Ricky cried out, "There it goes!" The children turned their heads to see the big canvas flying down a steep gully by the side of the road.

Mr. Hollister stopped the car. Pete opened the door and hopped out. Holly and Ricky begged to climb down the embankment for the tarpaulin, but their father selected Pete to go.

Digging his heels into the soft earth, the boy scrambled down the steep grade out of sight.

Five minutes passed but he did not return. Mrs. Hollister looked worried. "What do you suppose has happened to him?" she said.

Without a word, Mr. Hollister stepped out of the car. Ricky, Holly and Pam followed him. They peered over the edge of the deep gully. Pete was not in sight, but the tarpaulin lay far below in some tall cattails.

"Pete! Pete, where are you!" Pam called.

Over the howling of the wind they heard a muffled cry, and Ricky yelled, "The tarpaulin! I saw it move!"

CHAPTER 4

A WALKING HAT

"PETE's under the tarpaulin! I see his foot sticking out!" Ricky shouted as they scurried down the embankment.

With all hands grasping at the canvas, Ricky, Holly, Pam and Mr. Hollister unwrapped the struggling Pete. He got to his feet looking mussed up and embarrassed. He explained that a tricky wind had wrapped the canvas about him, pinning his arms to his sides. Then they all climbed back to the highway, where Pete and his father tied the tarpaulin securely over the luggage rack again.

On their way once more, the family noticed that the wind had subsided. "It looks as if we've missed the tornado after all," Mrs. Hollister said thankfully.

For many miles the children played a license plate game, trying to spy letters which would spell their names.

Sue won the contest and clapped gleefully. While Ricky complained that there were too many letters in his name, Mr. Hollister stopped in front of a small roadside restaurant and they all went in. Sue carried the box of cats, and set it under their table.

"Let's save some ice cream and milk for White

Nose and her kittens," Holly whispered to her younger sister.

When lunch was over and the waitress brought the check, Mr. Hollister sent Pete to the cashier to pay the bill. Ricky went with him.

"May we have our change in pennies?" Pete asked the woman at the cash register.

"Of course," she said pleasantly. "I have a lot of them today." She reached into the till and scooped up a handful of coins which she counted out to the two boys.

"Yikes, Pete!" Ricky said after he had examined the pennies. "We have two more for our collection."

"Oh, coin collectors," the woman said. "That's a nice hobby." She smiled and added, "I think I have something you'd like." She turned around to the shelf behind her and reached into a vase.

"Here," she said, "is an old Indian penny that I got in change over a year ago. How would you like to have it?"

"Crickets!" Pete exclaimed. "Thanks a million!"

While he and Ricky had been paying the bill, Sue and Holly had scrambled off their chairs and fed the cats part of their milk and ice cream.

A few minutes later Mr. Hollister opened the doors of the station wagon and called out, "All aboard!" Sue and Holly lifted the box of kittens into the car and the family piled in.

Just as her father was about to drive onto the road

again, Holly screamed, "Wait, Daddy!" Mr. Hollister jammed on the brakes so suddenly that everyone rocked forward.

"What's the matter?" Mrs. Hollister asked.

"There are only four kittens. One's missing!"

"Which one?" asked Ricky.

"It's Tutti-Frutti," Sue replied. "She must have jumped out of the box in the restaurant."

Mr. Hollister backed up, and everybody got out of the car to look for the missing kitten.

"My goodness," the cashier said as she saw them all troop back inside. "Didn't you have enough to eat?"

"We lost one of our cats," Pam said. "May we look for her?"

The woman smiled and said she would help. They looked under tables and chairs and behind the cashier's counter, but no Tutti-Frutti!

"She might have run into the kitchen," the waitress suggested.

"We'll look there," the cashier said.

The family followed her through swinging doors to see an array of shiny pots and pans. On one wall was a long stove on which a big kettle of soup was simmering.

"Chef," the cashier called out. "Have you seen a kitten in here?" A bald-headed man with a black moustache straightened up from behind one of the tables. He wore a white coat and apron but no hat.

44

"No, I didn't see a kitten, but I can't find my chef's hat, either."

"Maybe you dropped it in the soup," Holly suggested.

"Shush!" ordered Mrs. Hollister. "This is no time for jokes."

Quickly the children got on their hands and knees and crept around like cats themselves, all the while calling Tutti-Frutti's name.

Then Pam said, "I see your hat, Chef. It's over there under that table."

The chef hurried over and bent down to pick up the hat. He jumped back, startled. *The hat was moving along the floor!*

Ricky quickly sprang upon it, and, as he lifted it, there was Tutti-Frutti underneath!

Everybody laughed at the idea of the kitten wearing the chef's hat. Holly picked up the pet and cuddled her. The chef was happy to recover his hat and the children pleased to find Tutti-Frutti.

As the Hollisters drove along in their car once more, the children tried to figure out how the kitten got under the hat. Their guesses were interrupted by Mr. Hollister who pointed to a road sign, and said, "Glenco is the next town. We're pretty close to Crestwood."

"Let's stop at Glenco," Mrs. Hollister suggested, "and buy flowers for Aunt Marge." As Glenco was only a twenty-minute ride from their destination, Mr. Hollister agreed.

From the moment they reached the outskirts of the town, the Hollisters kept a sharp lookout for Joey Brill. "And if we should see him," Pam warned, "let's just make believe we didn't."

"Not me," Ricky said. "I'm going to make a face."

But as they drove through the center of town, no one saw the bully from Shoreham. Finally they stopped in front of a florist shop. As Mr. and Mrs. Hollister got out of the car, Pam followed.

"There's a phone booth down the street, dear," her mother said. "While Daddy and I buy the flowers, you telephone Aunt Marge to tell her we'll be there in a little while."

Pam ran down the street, took a coin from her pocket, stepped into the curbside booth and made the call to Crestwood.

"Aunt Marge!" Pam said gleefully, "we're in Glenco. We'll see you soon!"

Pam hung up, turned around and let out a cry of fright. Peering through the glass at her was Joey Brill! Beside him stood a smaller boy, about ten. He was thin and frail. Joey wore a mean grin as he barred the door.

"Let me out, Joey!" Pam cried, as she beat her fists on the glass. "Mother and Daddy are waiting for me."

"Oz and I saw you," Joey said, "while we were riding our bikes. Let your father go on without you!"

Pam cried out and beat on the door again, hoping

"Let me out, Joey!"

that her family would see or hear her. But there were several cars parked along the curb, obscuring the view of the telephone booth. In desperation Pam lunged at the door and in doing so, tore her dress.

"Let—me—out," she cried.

A man walking along the street stopped to see what the noise was about. When they saw him, Joey and Oz fled to their bicycles lying against the curb and pedaled off.

Pam hurried back to the car just as her mother and father stepped out of the florist shop carrying a white, neatly tied box of flowers.

When Pam told the others what had happened, Pete whistled. "Crickets, he's really in town. I guess we can expect more trouble."

"Don't worry," Mr. Hollister advised him. "At least Joey's not in Crestwood."

"I'll sew your dress, Pam, when we get to Aunt Marge's," Mrs. Hollister said.

They started off again, and after a few miles crossed the boundary of Crestwood. All the children cheered for their old home town. Mr. Hollister drove slowly, finally coming to the house where they used to live.

"Yikes, it hasn't changed a bit!" Ricky said as they passed it.

"Do you remember where cousin Teddy and Jean live?" Mrs. Hollister asked Sue.

"Way far away," replied the little girl, rolling her eyes.

"No, it's not that far," Ricky told her. "Their farm is on the other side of town, isn't it, Dad?"

"About five miles from here, I'd say," Mr. Hollister answered.

By this time the sky had clouded over again. They were still in Crestwood when a strange noise suddenly seemed to come from all directions.

"What's that?" Pam asked, as her father stopped the car to listen. He looked worried and his eyes scanned the sky. The noise grew louder, like the roar of a thousand locomotives.

Suddenly Pam pointed and screamed. Down the street the Hollisters saw the roof of a house peel off like a banana skin and fly through the air.

"A tornado!" Holly shrieked. "It's going to hit us!"

CHAPTER 5

THE TORNADO BOX

THE tornado had rushed upon them so suddenly that the Hollisters sat in terrified awe. Their station wagon bounced violently and slewed sideways in the street. Through the thunderous roar they could hear the sound of splitting branches as big trees toppled all about them.

Seconds later, the tornado had swirled off just as quickly as it had hit. Now, instead of being on a pleasant street lined with shade trees, the Hollisters sat in a jungle of leafy branches which nearly buried their car.

Nobody said anything for a few moments, then Mrs. Hollister's voice was heard. "Is anybody hurt?" she asked, glancing about at her children.

Pete and Pam lay sprawled on the seat while Ricky looked up dizzily from the floor. In the rear of the station wagon Holly sat up dazed, while Sue looked both frightened and comical with Cuddly and Midnight sitting on her head. When she reached up to remove the trembling kittens, the others laughed and the tension was eased.

"Phew!" Mr. Hollister said. "That was closer than I ever want to come to a tornado again."

Pete reached for the door handle, but his father

said quickly, "Everyone stay inside, there may be live wires or dangerous overhanging branches. We'll wait here until help comes."

As he spoke, Mrs. Hollister turned on their car radio and a voice said calmly, "This is Rescue Squad Headquarters broadcasting to all residents. If you are at home or in your cars, stay where you are. Help will soon be on its way. Repeat, do not go outdoors!"

Having recovered from the shock of their experience, the Hollisters studied the scene about them. Four large uprooted trees had boxed them in completely. A huge branch of one of the fallen giants hung menacingly over the roof of their car.

"Yikes, this is a keen adventure!" Ricky exclaimed. "Wait'll they hear about it back home."

The voices of the children were edged with excitement as they made jokes about their predicament.

After twenty minutes, Pam said, "If all the streets were hit as hard as this one, maybe we'll have to stay here all night."

"Uncle Russ and Aunt Marge must be terribly worried about us," Mrs. Hollister said.

A few minutes later, however, the buzzing of a power saw reached their ears.

"Hurray!" Pete cried out. "Help is on the way!"

Then through the leafy branches the Hollisters saw two trucks come into view. Four men, using two motor saws, stripped the large branches away. Then a tall thin man with a lean face and level gray eyes climbed over the debris and came to the side of the car. "Everybody in here okay?" he asked.

"Thank goodness, yes," Mr. Hollister replied.

"My name is Turner," the man introduced himself. "I'm the town forester. We'll get you out of this trap as quickly as possible."

Behind him another man climbed over a tree trunk. He wore a white helmet and leather jacket. When the children saw his face they gasped in astonishment.

"Uncle Russ!" they cried out together.

"Hi, brother," Mr. Hollister said, leaning out the window. "This is a fine way to greet your guests!"

"Well I'll be a monkey's uncle!" said Russ Hollister. He turned to the tree man and said, "Harry, this is my brother John and his family." Then, with a chuckle he went on, "Fancy meeting you here in the wilds of Crestwood!"

"But—but Uncle Russ," Holly said. "Did you give up being a cartoonist?"

"Of course not," came the laughing reply. "I'm a volunteer member of the Crestwood Rescue Squad."

"Yikes, that's keen!" Ricky blurted. "Will you let me wear your hat sometime?"

"Here, take it now." Russ Hollister handed the tin hat to his nephew, who put it on at a jaunty angle.

"How are Marge and the children?" Mrs. Hollister asked anxiously.

"They're well. Luckily the tornado missed our farm. The twister made a swath two blocks wide."

He turned to the tree man. "Any live wires down here, Harry?"

When Mr. Turner said that the area was safe, the children climbed out of the car.

"You can watch while we clear away the trees," the town forester told them. He and Uncle Russ manned a saw and began to cut through the trunk of the big elm directly blocking the path of the car.

"*Zing-ee, Zing-ee!*" sounded the saw as it cut through the thick wood. Finally the huge trunk fell apart, revealing many rings starting at the center of the trunk and spreading out to the bark. Holly and Ricky, who had climbed onto the hood of the car to watch the work, exclaimed in surprise.

"Haven't you ever seen the inside of a big tree before?" Mr. Turner asked.

When the children said no, he explained that the rings showed the age of the tree.

"Get busy and count these," Mr. Turner said with a grin, as he and Uncle Russ, together with two other workers, pulled the fallen elm to one side.

Pam, who was fastest at counting, completed the task first. "Sixty-seven rings, Mr. Turner," she said.

"That means the tree is sixty-seven years old," came the reply. "Older than any of us here."

Mr. Hollister stripped off his coat and joined Uncle Russ and two other rescue squad men in clearing up more of the debris.

Pete, meanwhile, received permission to help move some of the smaller branches. As he dragged them to the curb, he glanced into the roots of the largest overturned tree.

"Hey, what's this?" he asked, seeing an object caught among the twisted roots. He brushed away the clinging earth and tugged out an old metal box.

Ricky saw it. "Look what Pete found!" he exclaimed and ran over, followed by the girls.

"Where did you find it?" Pam inquired.

"What's inside?" Holly asked.

"Yikes!" Ricky said impatiently. "Let's open it!"

"I can't," replied Pete. "It's rusted shut." He held the box to his ear and shook it. "Something's rattling!" he exclaimed and carried the metal container to his father, Uncle Russ and Mr. Turner.

The forester examined their find. "Someone buried this years ago," he explained, "and the roots grew around it."

"Take it to our place," Uncle Russ said. "I have the proper tools there to open it."

Finally a path was cleared for the station wagon.

"I'll see you later," Uncle Russ said as he waved them on. "There's more work to be done before I come home."

"Here's your hat, Uncle Russ," Ricky said, and passed it through the rear window. "Thanks for letting me wear it."

"Good-by," Mr. Turner called out. "Come visit me at my office in the town hall. I'll show you my tree museum."

"Look what Pete found!" Ricky exclaimed.

"We will," Pam promised and waved to their new friend.

Mr. Hollister tested his motor. It was still in good working order, so he drove slowly through the littered streets to the outskirts of Crestwood. There he turned off on a small side road. After several miles he cut left into a lane bordered by a stone fence. Soon the Hollisters saw a rise of land where a pretty ranch-style house was nestled in a grove of trees. Behind it was an old barn and off to one side a modern-looking one-story building.

"That's Uncle Russ's new studio," Mrs. Hollister said. "He wrote to us about it."

Just then two children ran out of the house waving their arms and shouting a welcome. Teddy Hollister, eleven years old, had black hair and lively gray eyes. His sister Jean was nine. Her chestnut hair hung in a straight bob.

"Teddy, Jean!" Pam cried. As the car came to a halt, the children jumped out.

"I see Aunt Marge!" Holly declared. She ran across the lawn and flung herself into the arms of a pretty, slender woman who hurried to meet them.

"Oh dear, I'm glad you weren't hurt in that terrible tornado!" Aunt Marge said, leading her guests into the house.

"Uncle Russ saved us!" Ricky told her.

"And Mr. Turner, too," Holly declared. "A sixty-seven-year-old tree almost squashed us."

Sue trailed behind, carrying the box of flowers

which was nearly as large as she was. She presented them to her aunt.

"Oh, they're beautiful!" Aunt Marge said as she lifted the lid and pulled out a bouquet of yellow roses. "You're so thoughtful."

After the suitcases had been carried into the house, Pete got their penny collection to show his cousins.

"This sure is keen!" Teddy exclaimed, as he took a coin out of the album to study it.

"We have a piggy bank full of pennies," Jean said. "Let's open it!"

She hurried to her bedroom and returned with a large porcelain walrus.

"That's not a piggy bank," Ricky said scornfully.

"Well, it's a walrus piggy," Jean replied showing her dimples. She removed a cork from the underside of it. Out spilled dozens of pennies. The children quickly studied the dates on them.

"Ha!" Pete said. "Look, we have five more for our penny collection."

Meantime, Sue and Holly, having grown tired of looking at coins, explored the farm. While Holly peeked in the window of Uncle Russ's new studio, her little sister wandered behind the old barn.

Sue was out of sight only a few minutes when she returned on the run. Her face was flushed with excitement and she shouted breathlessly, "Help! Help! There's a lion behind the barn!"

CHAPTER 6

A TREASURE COIN

SUE dashed toward the house as fast as her chubby legs could carry her. "There's a big giant lion and he might eat me!" she screamed to the older children who had heard her cries and hurried out to see what was the matter.

As Holly ran up to them, Jean smiled and said, "All of you wait here with Teddy and I'll get the lion." She ran behind the barn and returned a minute later with the biggest dog the Hollisters had ever seen. He had a shaggy coat and a large head with floppy ears and kind-looking eyes.

"This is Leo, our new Saint Bernard dog," Jean said. "I don't blame you for thinking he was a lion."

"But—I heard him roar!" Sue said as she stepped forward, reached up and gingerly patted the dog's head. Leo gave a low growly bark and Sue jumped backward.

"Oh he won't hurt you," Teddy assured her. "Leo is only saying hello."

"What big sad eyes he has!" Pam said as the others admired the beautiful pet.

"Daddy got him for us six months ago," Teddy said. "I guess we forgot to tell you about him."

"Why did you name him Leo?" Pete asked.

"Because that means lion in the Latin language," Jean replied. "Mother thought it would be a good name."

"See! I told you he was a lion!" Sue declared.

"Well at least he's a tame one," Ricky said, and with an impish grin added, "Yikes, he's big enough to take a ride on!"

Ricky threw one leg over the dog's back as if mounting a horse, but Leo's fur was so slippery that the boy slid clear over and fell off on the other side. The cousins laughed and Leo did not seem to object. Instead he sat down so that red-faced Ricky could not straddle him again.

"Can he do any tricks?" Pam asked Teddy. Her cousin replied that Leo was too large to do any fancy tricks, but he could pull a dogcart.

"The only trouble is," Jean added, "sometimes he'll pull it and sometimes he won't."

"Depending on his mood," Teddy explained. He told the Hollisters that the dogcart was kept in the barn and used only on days when Leo felt especially frisky.

"Let's go see it now," said Ricky. As he moved away, Leo lumbered back toward his kennel behind the barn. At that moment a horn sounded in the driveway.

"Daddy's back!" Jean cried and ran to greet him.

"Hi, Uncle Russ!" Ricky cried as he ran up to the car. "Will you open that box for us now?"

The cartoonist said he would just as soon as he

changed from his rescue squad uniform. He strode toward the house in his coveralls and tin hat, which sat askew on his head. Aunt Marge greeted him at the door.

"Come in and say a proper hello to our guests," she said as they went into the living room.

"Tell us more about the tornado, Uncle Russ," Pete begged.

Aunt Marge took the tin hat as her husband flopped into an easy chair.

"Nobody hurt, thank goodness," the cartoonist said. "One man lost his wig, but we found it in a tree." The cousins laughed and he went on, "Lots of houses were damaged, though, and many trees uprooted."

"That's why we found the mysterious box," Pete said.

"Come on, Uncle Russ. Let's see what's in it," Holly urged him.

"Give your poor uncle time to catch his breath," Mrs. Hollister said.

"I'd like to find out what's in it too," Uncle Russ said, rising from the chair. He excused himself, changed his clothes, and, with the children trooping behind him, led the way to his workshop in one corner of the barn.

Along one side ran a long wooden workbench and above it on racks hung many kinds of tools. On the floor stood a wood lathe, which Uncle Russ used for making fancy chair legs, and a tall band saw. "This will cut metal," he explained.

Pete handed him the box and the children stood back while Uncle Russ started the motor which ran the saw. Soon the air vibrated with the humming of the flashing saw blade. Moments later the teeth whined through the metal box and the top fell off.

"Well, I'll be a monkey's uncle!" Uncle Russ said. "Look what's in the box!" He held up a round piece of metal for all to see. "It's an old coin."

"Crickets!" Pete cried out. "That looks like an Oak Tree shilling."

"A what?" Teddy asked.

The cartoonist gave Pete the coin to study more closely. "It sure *looks* like an Oak Tree shilling," he repeated. "What do you think, Pam? Remember, we read about it in that catalogue Mr. Steinberg gave us."

His sister held the coin in the palm of her hand, then turned it over. On one side was an oak tree and on the other the large date 1652. The letters around the edge were worn and indistinct. As Pam studied it, she remarked, "Look Pete, there are some letters hammered in around the oak tree. And a funny little figure is scratched beneath the date."

"Let's go inside and study it with a magnifying glass," Uncle Russ suggested.

"It looks as if we've run into another mystery," Ricky said as they hurried into the house.

Pam immediately went to get the catalogue while

Jean fetched a large magnifying glass. When they returned to the living room, Mr. and Mrs. Hollister and Aunt Marge were examining the strange coin. Pete's father handed it to him.

"We're all curious to know what it is," he said.

Pete took the glass and carefully compared the coin to the picture of an Oak Tree shilling in the catalogue. "We were right!" he said triumphantly. "This was made in Massachusetts more than three hundred years ago!"

Pam quickly told the others the history of the old coin. She explained that the first money used in Massachusetts was wampum, but in 1652 the colonists began minting coins. The Oak Tree shilling was among the earliest made.

"They continued to mint these shillings for about thirty years, using the same date," Pam concluded.

"How fascinating!" Aunt Marge exclaimed. "I can see now why you're so interested in coin collecting."

"You learn lots of history that way," Pam replied.

"And old secrets too," Pete declared. "Look here, for instance. Whoever hid this coin under the old tree put a message on it."

"What? Where?" Holly asked. "Let me look."

Pete passed the magnifying glass to her and she studied the oak tree carefully. "See those letters hammered around the tree?" Pete asked.

"Yes, I see them," his sister replied. "There's a word—t-r-e-a-s-u-r-e."

62

"Treasure!" Jean cried out. "This must be a clue to where it's hidden."

"Yikes!" exclaimed Ricky. "Pirates!"

"Not only that," Pete said as he turned the coin over, "but look at the other side." He handed the coin to his uncle. Beneath the number "2" and alongside the Roman numeral "XII" was scratched a crude figure of a flying bird.

"Now what do you think this is all about?" Uncle Russ asked. He shook his head and laughed. "Every time we see you Shoreham Hollisters there's a mystery to be solved!"

"I think Jean's guess is right," Mrs. Hollister said. "The coin must be a message about some sort of treasure."

"If it is," Uncle Russ remarked, "whatever happened was so long ago that the answer is probably gone forever."

"Don't be too sure, Daddy," Jean said. "We've solved mysteries before, you know."

Pete suggested that they show Mr. Turner the coin on their visit to him at the Town Hall.

"That's a good place to start our detective work," Pam agreed.

"Let's go first thing in the morning," Ricky said, jumping up eagerly.

"Not tomorrow," Holly reminded him. "It's Sunday."

"Monday then," Ricky said and turned a somersault.

After the younger children had gone to bed, Pete, Pam and their cousins pored over the coin catalogue.

At bedtime Teddy said, "I think you've made a coin bug out of me."

"Good!" Pam said cheerily. "Now we'll have more to write each other about."

After saying her prayers, Pam went to sleep thinking of the mysterious Oak Tree shilling. In her dreams the bare branches of the tree moved like giant gnarled fingers and when they clutched her shoulder, she awakened with a start. Opening her eyes, she saw that Sue's little hand was shaking her.

"Come on, let's get up and ride in the dogcart," Sue whispered to her.

Pam yawned, stretched, hopped out of bed and looked out the window. Mr. Hollister and his brother were just stepping from the car with the Sunday newspapers. At that moment there was a knock on the door and Jean came in. "Daddy's back from town with the funnies," she said. "Let's hurry and get dressed."

The two cousins helped Sue into her starched pinafore, put on their clothes and hurried downstairs.

The entire household was stirring, and the aroma of frying bacon sharpened everyone's appetite. At the breakfast table Mrs. Hollister warned her children to stay clean, at least until after they got back from church.

"We leave in half an hour," Mr. Hollister said, rising from the table and glancing at his wrist watch.

Ricky, Holly and Sue sat on the living room sofa and quickly read the comics. Then the red-headed boy became restless. He caught the attention of Sue and Holly and with a slight motion of his head beckoned them outside.

"Let's hitch up the dogcart," Ricky said when he was out of earshot of the others. "You get Leo," he told the girls, "while I open the barn door."

Sue and Holly found Leo lounging in his kennel, his big head resting on his paws halfway out the door. "Come on, Leo!" Sue urged, running up and pulling him by the collar. "We're going for a ride."

Leo reluctantly lumbered to his feet. With Sue pulling and Holly pushing, he was coaxed to the barn door which now stood open. Ricky found the dogcart and wheeled it out. It looked like a pony cart they once had used in Shoreham, but it was smaller. Its harness was much the same, however, and soon Ricky had Leo standing between the two shafts. When the leather belts were buckled into place, he invited his two sisters to step inside the cart.

"Be careful, Sue," Holly warned. "Don't get mussed up."

"Let's ride up the hill and down again," Ricky suggested.

As he pulled Leo by the collar, the big dog plod-

They coaxed Leo toward the barn.

ded along. Holly held the reins, and her face shone with excitement. When they reached the foot of the hill, however, the Saint Bernard stopped.

"Come on, boy. I'll give you a dog biscuit!" Ricky bribed.

"I think we're too heavy to pull uphill," Holly said as she and Sue hopped down from the cart.

The shaggy dog gave a growly bark as if to say thank you, then pulled the cart to the top of the grassy hill in back of the barn. The three children ran after him.

"Now we can all ride down together!" Ricky said. He squeezed into the cart between his sisters and called "giddap!" But the big dog would not move. Instead he sat down.

"Oh, come on, Leo," Ricky chided him. "Be a good sport and pull us down the hill."

But Leo apparently had no thoughts of such exertion on a Sunday morning.

"All right then, I'll pull you," Ricky told his sisters. He unharnessed Leo. The dog trotted down the hill and made straight for his kennel, where he lay down with his head sticking out in the sun.

Ricky stepped between the shafts and said, "Now watch me. I'll make believe I'm Leo." Ricky threw back his head and barked. Then he picked up the shafts and started down the hill.

The two girls cried out with delight as the cart sped over the green grass. Ricky's strides grew longer and he ran faster. Suddenly he felt that the dogcart was starting to go faster than he was.

"It's going to run over me!" Ricky thought wildly. "What'll I do?"

CHAPTER 7

THE WISHING FOUNTAIN

As THE dogcart sped down the hill, Holly and Sue realized that Ricky was in trouble. They were too frightened to cry out, but hung on tightly to the sides of the cart. Exhausted, Ricky could stretch his legs no farther. He must do something, and quickly!

Near the foot of the hill sloped a field of tall white daisies. "There!" Ricky thought in a flash. "The daisies will make a soft spot if the girls fall out of the cart."

Quickly the boy dropped the shafts and flung himself flat on the grass. The dogcart passed over him without touching and careened toward the daisy field.

The shafts now bumped along the ground, and the cart swayed and zigzagged. With one big lurch Holly and Sue were thrown head over heels into the daisy field. The wagon kept on down the hill and stopped not far from Leo's kennel.

Ricky picked himself up and raced madly after the two girls. They rolled over and over in the flowers and finally stopped, their hair and dresses full of daisy petals.

"Are you all right?" Ricky shouted as he ran up to them.

Sue stood up, walked backward in circles and plopped down into the daisies again. "I'm dizzy," she said.

Holly threw her pigtails back over her shoulders, brushed off her dress and picked up Sue. Then the three looked at one another shamefacedly.

"Oh, there are green stains on your white shirt!" Holly said, pointing to her brother.

"Ha-ha. You should see the back of your dress," Ricky said. "It's all green too."

There was a hole in Sue's pinafore and her black hair was mussed up.

"Ricky, that was a good ride!" Sue said, when suddenly Holly pointed to the dogcart.

Sitting in it was Leo himself.

"Maybe *he* wants a ride like that!" Holly said with a giggle as they raced over to the Saint Bernard.

"Yikes, Pete and Pam would like to see this!" Ricky declared. He grasped one of the shafts while his sisters took hold of the other. Together they pulled the cart toward the back of the house. As they rounded the corner of the barn they saw both families assembled, ready to step into their cars and go to church.

"Oh-oh!" said Ricky softly.

Mrs. Hollister was the first to spy them. "Oh, my goodness!" she cried. "What has happened to you? I told you to stay clean!"

"Look, we're giving Leo a ride," Ricky said, trying to appear unconcerned.

"We went for a dogcart ride," Holly said.

"And something happened," Sue chimed in.

"I'll say it did!" Mr. Hollister declared.

Uncle Russ put a hand up to his face so that the children could not see him smiling. "I could use this in my comic strip," he said aside to his brother.

"Come with me," Mrs. Hollister ordered the younger children. "You'll have to wash and change your clothes." She took Sue by the hand and led the way into the house.

"I'm sorry, Mother," Ricky said as he followed. "It's all my fault."

"It's my fault, too—a little bit," said Holly.

"But Leo didn't get hurt," Sue declared happily.

Pete and Pam helped to wash and dress the mischievous youngsters and soon they were all on their way to church.

Later, at the dinner table Uncle Russ saw that Ricky, Holly and Sue remained unusually quiet. While they were eating ice cream for dessert he said brightly, "I have something that would interest you coin collectors—a box of gold coins."

The youngsters' eyes grew large with excitement.

"Gold coins?" Pete said. "They must be ancient!"

Uncle Russ rose from the table, went into the living room and returned with a box in his hands. He opened it, reached in and put a gold coin in front of each of the children.

"Yikes!" Ricky said as he examined the bit of gold. Then he declared, "Uncle Russ, you're fooling us."

Holly giggled and Sue started laughing. The gold coins Uncle Russ had given them were after-dinner mints wrapped with gold foil.

Seeing that the younger children were jolly again, Uncle Russ passed the candies to the adults. As he nibbled on a chocolate mint, he went on, "But I do have a bag of coins somewhere around the house. I collected them when I was a boy." He turned to his wife, "Marge, do you know where they are?"

"They're in the storage room, I think," she said, licking a bit of chocolate from the tip of her finger. "Perhaps the boys can look for them after dinner."

While the girls helped to clear the table, Pete, Teddy and Ricky entered the storeroom. In it were several old trunks, and many crates and cartons.

"What box do we look for?" Pete asked.

Teddy said his mother told him there was a carton marked "Dad's treasures." "It's all the junk he used to collect when he was young like us," Teddy declared.

The boys went from box to box, looking at the writing on each one. There were cartons marked "doll clothes," "old dresses," "Jean's first-grade drawings," and "pictures." Finally, at the bottom of a stack of cartons, Teddy found the one they were looking for. Carefully the boys pulled it out, opened the top and looked inside.

"Jimminy!" Teddy exclaimed. "I didn't know Dad had saved all this stuff!"

The box contained several old roller skate wheels,

school notebooks, a scout knife, a whistle carved from a tree twig and a leather bag closed at the neck by a stout thong. Ted picked it up and shook it, but as he did the thong came loose and over the wooden floor scattered an avalanche of marbles.

"Yikes, wrong bag!" Ricky said and the three boys scrambled to retrieve the rolling marbles. Ricky skidded on one and plunged headlong into a stack of cardboard boxes which fell on him. One broke open and the freckle-faced boy looked up from the floor grinning, with three frilly doll dresses draped over his head.

"Let's find those coins and get out of here," Ricky said, "before something else happens."

When the marbles had been replaced and the doll clothes stuffed back, the three cousins rummaged deeper into the carton. Pete found a smaller sack made of canvas. He pulled it out along with a yellowed envelope.

"These are the coins, all right," Pete said as he looked inside the sack.

"Say, what's that?" Teddy asked, taking the envelope from his cousin. He held it near the light of a window and said, "Oh-oh, it's one of Daddy's report cards." He slipped it quickly into his pocket.

The three boys returned to the living room. The girls had finished their chores and were eager to see the old coins. Pete emptied the bag onto the rug and the cousins flopped down to examine them.

Included in the find were several Lincoln head

"Yikes, the wrong bag!"

pennies which the Hollisters did not have in their coin book. The rest of the old money was of no extra value.

Teddy studied the catalogue and exclaimed, "Say, here's a penny worth four hundred dollars. I wish we had one of them."

"Oh, that's the Flying Eagle cent," Pam remarked. "I was wishing Uncle Russ would have one!"

"Speaking of wishes," Uncle Russ said, "something new has been added to Crestwood since you moved away."

"Oh goody, what is it?" Holly asked.

"We have a fountain now in front of the Town Hall. It's nicknamed the 'wishing fountain.'" Uncle Russ explained that if coins were thrown into the water, wishes were supposed to come true. "But don't throw in any valuable old coins," he added laughingly.

Aunt Marge told them that at the end of each year the money was taken out of the fountain and used to provide turkey and toys for poor children at Christmas.

"Let's go see the fountain and make some wishes," Pam suggested eagerly.

"You can ride into town with me if you like," said Uncle Russ. "I have some cartoons I want to mail."

"Use my station wagon," Mr. Hollister urged his brother. "Elaine and I will go with Marge to call on our old friends, the Joyces."

"I'll get my camera," Pete said, "and take a picture of the wishing fountain."

A few minutes later he joined the other children in the station wagon and Uncle Russ drove into town. The debris left by the tornado had been carted away. Some trees lining the street still were tilted far to one side, but the loose twigs and branches had been removed.

"I want to put these cartoons in the mailbox in front of the Post Office," Uncle Russ said as he parked the car. "You children go ahead. I'll meet you there." The cousins walked the two blocks to the Town Hall.

"Oh, how beautiful!" Pam exclaimed as they came in sight of the wishing fountain.

Jets of water sprayed into the air from the top of a stone platter mounted on a pile of artistically arranged rocks. Around the base of the fountain lay a large pool of water about a foot deep. Several people were throwing coins into the pool.

Pam noticed a poorly dressed man peer into the water as if he had lost something. He wore khaki trousers and a blue work shirt with a frayed collar. His hair was thick and blond with streaks of gray through it. His nose was large and his eyes had a sad look.

Pam walked over to him. "Did you lose something, sir? If you did, I'll help you find it."

The man jerked his head up as if startled and

76

looked at Pam. Then he hurried away without a word.

The other children, meanwhile, were skipping around the rim of the fountain. A breeze blew some of the spray on Holly and she laughed gaily.

"I'd like to get a close-up picture of those rocks," Pete said to himself. He stepped up onto the rim of the fountain and focused his camera.

Suddenly Ricky shouted, "Pete! Look out! Joey Brill!"

CHAPTER 8

CANNONBALL HOLLY

HEARING the warning shout, Pete stepped quickly to one side and whirled around, nearly dropping his camera in the water. Joey Brill, who had run up behind him, shoved nothing but empty air.

The force almost carried the bully into the water, but he stopped short, his face red with embarrassment. Then he shouted, "Come on, Oz. These Hollisters are too stuck-up to play with, anyhow."

Only then did the children notice another boy with Joey. He was about ten years old, thin, frail and stoop-shouldered. His eyes looked frightened. Joey beckoned to him and ran around the other side of the fountain. The boy named Oz followed, looking back over his shoulder as if fearful that the Hollisters might hurt him.

Pete quickly handed his camera to Sue, and dashed after the bully. Ricky and Holly, too, took up the chase. Oz panted along behind Joey, and just as Pete was about to catch up with the two, they raced into a parking lot, flung themselves into a car and locked the door.

"If you want to wrestle fair, come on out," Pete called.

Joey merely stuck out his tongue, pressed his

thumbs against his head and waggled his fingers. "You can't get us!" he cried with a smirk.

"You're both fraidy cats!" Holly said indignantly.

The three Hollister children turned back and came face to face with a stout woman who looked very determined.

"What's going on here?" she demanded, walking up to the car door. Joey opened it.

"They're the Hollisters from Shoreham, Aunt Thelma," he declared, "and they're trying to get Oz."

"Oh, that's a big fib!" Holly declared.

Pete shushed his sister, introduced himself to the woman, and told the correct story of what had happened.

"I'm Mrs. Thelma Brill," the woman said. "Joey is my nephew and Osmer is my son." She explained that Joey was staying with them while his parents went to a convention.

"We wouldn't hurt Oz," Pete said. "He didn't do anything to us."

Mrs. Brill looked sternly at Joey. "I told both of you not to leave the car while I was on my errand," she said. "If you had minded me, there would have been no trouble."

Pete said he was sorry that they had made Oz run so fast. Although frightened, he seemed like a nice boy.

Mrs. Brill said good-by, and the Hollisters hurried back to the fountain.

"Yikes!" Ricky said as they hurried along. "What a cousin Joey must be!"

"Too bad Osmer doesn't have relatives like Teddy and Jean," Holly piped up.

As they turned the corner of the square before the Town Hall, Ricky and Holly noticed an old cannon across the street from the fountain. They ran over to look at the relic while Pete returned to the others. As Sue gave him the camera, Pete told the girls what had happened.

"I feel sorry for Oz," said kindhearted Pam. "He looked so scared!"

"I hope he doesn't believe any of those wild stories that Joey will tell him about us," Jean said.

Pete took several pictures of the fountain, one of them of the girls tossing pennies and making wishes.

"I wish you would come to visit us more often," Jean said, as her penny plopped into the water.

Pam wished that Joey would not mistreat Oz, and Teddy hoped for a big adventure while his cousins were in Crestwood.

Pam gave Sue a penny, and when the coin flew from her chubby hand, she declared, "I want a dog like Leo to play with Zip."

Meanwhile, across the street, Ricky and Holly stood looking up at the old cannon. Off to one side was a mound of cannon balls. Ricky tried to lift one off the top of the heap but to his embarrassment found that they were all welded together.

"Were you going to try to shoot it?" asked Holly, twirling one of her pigtails.

Ricky shrugged and thrust his hands deep into his pockets. Then he grinned and said, "We ought to be able to play some kind of a game with it."

"Remember at a circus one time we saw a lady shot from a cannon?" Holly asked. "We could play that."

"Just make-believe."

"Of course, silly, there isn't any net to catch me in."

Before Ricky could say yes or no, Holly scrambled up to the black barrel of the cannon. Then grasping it tightly with arms and legs, she inched her way to the muzzle.

She turned her head to look back to Ricky. "I think I could get my legs into it," she called gleefully.

"Yikes, that would be keen," Ricky said. "Then I could make-believe set off the cannon and *phoom*, you could make-believe fly through the air."

"But I can't get inside of this alone," Holly told her brother. "Come help me, Ricky."

Ricky ran to a spot beneath the muzzle of the cannon. Standing on tiptoes, he helped Holly fit her legs inside the gaping black hole.

Holly slid in clear up to her waist.

"All right, Ricky," she commanded, "shoot the cannon!"

Ricky ran to the back, pretended to fire it, then shouted, "Kerboom!"

His voice carried across the street to the other children at the fountain.

"For goodness' sakes!" Pam cried out in alarm. "*Look* at Holly!"

"Let's get her out of there," Pete said. "She might get hurt."

With Sue trotting behind, the older children hurried to the cannon.

"Watch," Holly said, as she flailed her arms like a bird, "I'm flying through the air."

"All right, you've had your game," Pete replied. "Get down out of there. Uncle Russ will be back soon."

Pete and Teddy reached up to grasp Holly's outstretched hands.

"One-two-three-pull!" Pete said.

Holly did not budge.

The boys pulled again.

"Ouch, you're pulling my arms off!" Holly complained. "I'm stuck!"

Hearing this, Ricky climbed out on the cannon, and tried pulling his sister's shoulders, but this did not work either. Holly was lodged tightly in the barrel of the cannon!

Hearing the children's shouts of dismay, a group of grownups quickly gathered to help. At that moment, Uncle Russ appeared and his eyes popped

"I'm flying through the air," said Holly.

when he saw his niece. But even he and the by-standers could not free Holly.

"Maybe we'll just have to blow her out like they do in the circus," Ricky said with a big sigh.

Holly did not know whether to laugh or cry, but she decided to be brave as Uncle Russ said, "I guess we'll have to call the fire department."

"Please don't let them squirt water on me!" Holly pleaded. "I'll be good."

Quick as a monkey, Ricky hopped down from the cannon, ran to the corner and pulled the fire alarm. Two minutes later, with sirens wailing, the fire trucks arrived in the town square. Uncle Russ greeted them with a wry smile. "One girl stuck in a cannon," he said, shaking his head.

"Well, at least it's not a cat in a tree," one of the firemen declared. Then he called to a man with a silver badge on his hat, "Chief, what would you suggest we do?"

The fire chief ordered one of his men to bring a small extinguisher from one of the trucks. "This is a foamy soapy fluid," he said. "I think it will turn the trick."

While Holly looked more frightened than amused, the fire chief pushed a small nozzle into the cannon between Holly's back and the cold metal.

Squish-squish-squish! The foamy stuff squirted all about her.

"Ooh, it's cold!" Holly cried out.

"But it's wet and slippery," the fire chief said. He

put the extinguisher down, then grasped Holly's arms while the crowd looked on expectantly. Holly slipped from the mouth of the cannon like a watermelon seed from a boy's fingers.

"There you are, little lady," the fire chief said, setting her on the grass. "Let's stay out of cannons from now on, shall we?"

Holly nodded yes, but she was so embarrassed that she raced off toward the station wagon.

"This is the second time she's been messed up today," Ricky said importantly. "These girls, tsk, tsk."

With her chin quivering, Holly sat on the floor of the back seat all the way home. When she stepped out of the car, Pam and Jean went with her to the guest room, and closed the door.

"Don't worry, honey," Pam said kindly. "We'll get you in a shower and you'll be good as new."

"From now on your name is Cannonball Holly," Jean said with a twinkle in her eyes.

A tear ran down alongside Holly's nose. She sniffled but had to laugh at her cousin's joke. "I don't ever want to be a cannonball again," she said.

By the time Holly had been cleaned up and the three girls went to the living room Mr. and Mrs. Hollister and Aunt Marge had returned. Ricky was first to blurt out the story of his sister's mishap.

"And you helped her get into the cannon," Mrs. Hollister said, shaking her head reprovingly. "You children certainly have been up to mischief today."

"It seems to me," Uncle Russ said with a wink, "that youngsters get into more scrapes today than we ever did."

Teddy quickly spoke up. "You mean you never were naughty, Daddy?" he asked.

"Of course not. Hardly ever," he said, grinning at his brother.

"Well, I hate to disappoint you, Dad," Teddy remarked as he reached into his pocket and pulled out the yellowed piece of paper. "I found this report card in the storeroom."

Uncle Russ looked surprised. "Mine?"

"Yes," Teddy said. "The grades on it weren't bad, but—" and he turned the card over, "there's a note from your teacher on the back."

"Oh, let's hear it!" Aunt Marge said with an impish smile.

In a very serious voice, Teddy read:

"'Please speak to Russell and his brother John. They have been annoying the girls by pulling their pigtails.'"

The laughter that followed could be heard nearly to the fountain in Crestwood!

CHAPTER 9

DETECTIVE WORK

AFTER the laughter had died down, Mrs. Hollister forgave her children, saying that they must take after their father and Uncle Russ. This remark put everyone in a jolly mood again and the children joked about it until supper.

Afterward, the cousins spent the evening playing games around the dining room table. Aunt Marge gave the girls permission to make popcorn and pink lemonade which they served just before bedtime.

"Let's make plans for tomorrow," Pam said after the younger children had gone to undress.

"I think the four of us should do some detective work in town alone," Pete suggested.

"That's right," Teddy agreed. "We have to see Mr. Turner, the tree man, and visit the coin shop. Perhaps we can learn something more about the Oak Tree shilling."

Before going to bed the cousins obtained permission from their parents to ride the bus into Crestwood the next day.

On Monday morning, Pete, Pam, Teddy and Jean rose early, finished breakfast quickly, and set off down the road to meet the bus. After a few minutes' wait, it came along. Because the route was over country roads, the bus was dusty.

"Crickets, it really needs a bath!" Pete said as the vehicle drew near.

"It's always that way," Jean said. "That's why the driver's nickname is Dusty."

With squeaking brakes, the bus came to a stop, the door swung open, and a husky voice called out cheerfully, "All aboard for Crestmont-Crestview-Crestwood-Crust-of-bread, or whatever the name of that town is!"

As the children stepped into the bus, they were greeted by the driver. He had a ruddy face, crew-cut gray hair, and smile-crinkled eyes.

"I'm glad to see you brought your mother and father along today," he said, speaking to Teddy.

"Oh, Dusty, quit your kidding," Jean said. "These are our cousins, Pete and Pam."

"Glad to meet you," Dusty replied as he swung the door shut and started off again.

"How much is the fare, Dusty?" Pete asked.

"Two dimes and a nickel; for you twenty-five cents."

The cousins deposited their coins, and as they walked back to sit down, Pam turned to the driver, "When does your bus leave Crestwood, Dusty?"

He grinned. "Mondays, Wednesdays, and Fridays quarter after the hour; all other days, fifteen minutes past."

Twenty minutes later the bus stopped near the

Town Hall. The children said good-by to Dusty and stepped off.

Crestwood bustled with Monday morning activity. Pete suggested that they go first to the coin shop, and Teddy led the way around the corner and two blocks up the main street. The place they entered was a combination old book and coin store. Pete went directly to the proprietor, a slender man with dark hair and a pleasant smile.

"May I help you?" he asked. "Would you like to buy some books?"

Pete reached into his pocket and pulled out the mysterious coin. "We'd like some information about this Oak Tree shilling," he said. The man took it and examined it with a short tube-like magnifying glass which he held to his eye.

"This *is* an Oak Tree shilling," he said, "but it doesn't have much value. You see, it's been defaced."

"That's what I wanted to ask about," Pete said. "Do you suppose those funny marks were put on in Colonial days?"

"I think not," the man replied. "Those letters and this odd bird probably were the work of a prankster." Then he stroked his chin thoughtfully. "Hmm," he said, "of course, there may be a hidden meaning."

"That's just what we thought," Pam said eagerly.

"Sorry I can't help you," came the reply. The man handed back the coin.

The children thanked him and left.

The next stop was the Town Hall, where they found Mr. Turner's office in a large basement room. The forester was seated behind a desk on the far side of the room. A long, low table stood against the opposite wall. On it were dozens of odd-looking pieces of tree trunks and branches.

"Good morning, children," the man said, rising. "I see you'd like to know some more about trees."

"Oh yes, Mr. Turner," Pam said. "Trees are fun, especially when they provide a mystery."

"How's that?" the forester asked, and Pete told him about the mysterious coin they had found in the box from the uprooted oak.

"Trees are mysterious, all right," their host agreed. "But that's not surprising because they are like people."

When Teddy looked skeptical, the forester went on, "Take an oak on a tree farm, it starts as a small acorn, which the farmer washes and plants in warm earth. When the baby tree sprouts and grows taller it is transplanted into a field. Just as two children can be the same age, but different sizes, two trees may be equal in age, but one can be larger or perhaps healthier than the other. Like people, trees have skin—that's the bark, and their blood is sap. And trees can get sick," Mr. Turner added.

"Are there tree doctors?" Jean asked, smiling.

"That's right," the man replied. "They give the trees vitamins and special foods. Just as a child must have his fingernails and hair cut," he went on, "trees have to be trimmed."

"I guess trees are our friends," Pam said.

"I never thought too much about it," Jean ventured.

"If there were no trees there wouldn't be any forests," Pam went on. "No place for birds to nest or wild animals to roam."

"Not only that," Mr. Turner agreed, "trees hold the top soil with their roots."

"And mysterious boxes, too!" Teddy declared.

"That's not unusual," Mr. Turner said. "Come here, and I'll show you the things that trees have had hidden in them." He led them over to the table, which contained his exhibits. There he pointed out cross sections of four tree trunks: in the first could be seen a piece of barbed wire, in the second, a clothes-line pulley, in the third, an old gate hinge, and in the last, the nose of a bullet.

"Crickets!" Pete exclaimed. "How do these things get inside of trees?"

Mr. Turner explained that in many cases, like the gate hinge or the barbed wire, the object was attached to the tree, which, in time, grew right around it.

"What's this?" Teddy asked curiously and pointed to a small swollen limb which resembled a rat with a tail.

"A branch," the forester said. "They grow into strange formations sometimes. Look at this." He showed them another limb resembling an owl with large hollow eyes. With a grin he pressed a button on the side of the table and the owl's eyes lighted up green. The girls giggled.

"Look," said Pete, "here's a perfect cane! The branch just grew that way."

"I never knew trees were so interesting," Jean remarked when they had finished looking at all the odd pieces which Mr. Turner had collected.

"They're useful, too," the man said. "Think about the Pilgrims. They came in boats made of wood, cut down trees to build cabins and churches and used the branches for firewood. They made furniture, even cradles, knives, forks, and spoons from wood. Flat dishes, too.

"They filled cloth bags with pine needles for pillows. Shredded bark was used to stuff mattresses and from white birch bark they made paper. Besides, there were berries for ink. Bows and arrows were made of wood, and twisted pieces of bark were used for string."

"Golly!" Teddy remarked. "No wonder you like trees so much, Mr. Turner."

The man smiled and went to his desk where he picked up a small paper box, opened it, and offered it to the children.

"Here's one of the nicest things made from trees."

"Oh," Pam cried, "maple sugar candy!"

"Help yourself," Mr. Turner said, and the children munched on the sweet confection.

The girls giggled when the owl's eyes glowed.

"There's another secret I'll let you in on," the forester confided. "Chewing gum is made from the sap of spruce trees."

"Crickets!" Pete said, "Can you imagine chewing a tree!"

Pam reminded her brother that he had not come to town to make jokes, but to do some sleuthing about the mysterious coin.

Pete grew serious again and asked Mr. Turner who owned the house where the uprooted tree had stood.

"Some people named Gordon, I believe," came the reply. "Are you going to visit them?"

"Yes," Pete said. "Perhaps they know something about that old box we found."

The four cousins thanked Mr. Turner for his hospitality, and left his cool basement office. When they came out in front of the Town Hall they paused in the morning sunlight to plan their next move.

"Suppose Pete and I go to see the Gordons," Teddy suggested.

"All right," his sister agreed. She turned to Pam, "We have a new super department store in Crestwood since you left. Let's go see it."

Pam was delighted with the idea, and they agreed to meet the boys at the store for lunch later.

Pete and Teddy walked to the place where the elm had fallen. They found that most of the trunk had been sawed up and carted away. But the old root still lay on its side next to the big hole in which it had stood. After the boys had gazed into the hollow, they walked up the front steps of the house and rang the doorbell. An elderly man answered.

"Are you Mr. Gordon?" Pete asked.

"Yes, what can I do for you boys?"

"We'd like to ask you some questions about that old tree," Pete said.

"Come on in," Mr. Gordon said cordially.

Mrs. Gordon was sitting in the living room. Her husband introduced her to Pete and Teddy.

Pete told the couple about finding the box and the Oak Tree shilling, but neither the man nor his wife had any idea of how the box had got into the tree roots.

"We've lived here for many years," Mrs. Gordon said. "The tree was quite tall when we moved in."

"Who owned the house before that?" Pete asked.

"Mr. Eli Spencer. He sold it to us at the time he bought his big estate."

"Oh, that's near our place," Teddy said. "Old Mr. Spencer died, but his son lives there now. We can go see him."

"Is his father the one who left the coin collection to the museum?" Pete asked.

Mr. Gordon nodded. "The same one."

The boys thanked the elderly couple for the information, then hurried to the department store where they met their sisters in the shiny new cafeteria.

When Pam heard their story, she said, "One clue leads to another. Perhaps Mr. Spencer's son can tell us about the mysterious coin and what it means."

After a luncheon of sandwiches and milk, the four decided to look at the Eli Spencer coin collection before going back to the farm.

Crestwood's library and museum were contained in the same building on the opposite side of the square from the Town Hall. Pam and Jean giggled as they passed the cannon where Holly had been stuck and Pete rolled his eyes at the thought of the episode.

"It's lucky Ricky and Holly weren't arrested," he said in a mock grown-up tone, as they crossed the street to the museum. In front of the building stood two police cars and a small knot of people, peering into the front door.

"Oh dear," Pam said, "do you suppose somebody's been hurt inside?"

"Nobody's been hurt," one of the onlookers remarked.

"What happened then?" Pete asked.

"A coin collection was stolen," a woman explained, "while the custodian was out for lunch."

"How dreadful!" Jean cried, just as four policemen came down the steps of the building.

"Don't go away, any of you!" ordered one of them who wore a sergeant's stripes.

"What do you mean, officer?" Teddy asked.

"We want to question and search everyone in the vicinity," he said. "That coin collection was very valuable!"

"But we just got here," Pam said.

"Turn out your pockets, everybody!" the sergeant ordered, ignoring her.

Pete pulled out his wallet, some loose change and the Oak Tree shilling. As he did, a husky policeman stepped over and examined the money.

"Sergeant!" he called sharply and his hand closed on Pete's shoulder. "Here's a boy who has an old coin!"

CHAPTER 10

A *FISHHOOK CLUE*

PETE was dumfounded when the policeman took the old coin from his hand.

"Where are the rest of them?" the officer asked sternly.

"But-but," Pete stammered, so amazed he could hardly speak.

"My brother didn't steal that coin from the museum," Pam spoke up. "We weren't even in there."

"That's right, officer," Teddy came to his cousin's defense. "The old coin really belongs to us."

"Well, we can settle that quickly enough," the policeman declared as he saw a tall, slender man in a sports jacket striding briskly along the sidewalk.

"Oh, Mr. Spencer!" the officer called. "Over here, please. I think we may have a clue."

"That's Mr. Eric Spencer, old Eli's son," Jean whispered. "He's the one who lives near us."

The man hurried over to the officer and said, "Sergeant Costello, what's this I hear about my father's coin collection being stolen. I came over as soon as I got word of it."

"That's right," the sergeant replied, "and this boy may have one of the coins."

"But he's our cousin!" Jean cried out. "You know

us, Mr. Spencer. We're Russell Hollister's children."

"Oh yes," the man replied with a quick smile.

"And these are our cousins who used to live in Crestwood," she added, nodding to Pete and Pam.

"I hardly think these children would take anything from the museum," Mr. Spencer said. "Here, let me look at the coin."

He examined it carefully, then shook his head. "No, this is not from my father's collection. It's an old piece, all right. What does that word 'treasure' mean? And the picture of that odd-looking bird?"

"That's what we're trying to find out, Mr. Spencer," Pete said. "We'd like to talk to you about it sometime. May we?"

"Certainly. After all this excitement is over, you bring your coin to my house."

Pete thanked the man for helping him. Then the sergeant apologized and hastened into the building with Eric Spencer.

"Let's go in and do some sleuthing ourselves," Pete said, "now that I'm no longer a suspect."

Several of the onlookers laughed at Pete's remark, and the four children entered the building. The policemen were busy searching here and there for any clue the thief might have left.

Entering the room where the coins had been stolen, the children looked about. In the center stood a large glass case. The lid had been raised and policemen were dusting the glass for fingerprints.

"I think the lock on the case has been picked,

Sergeant," one of the officers told his superior. "There are some sharp scratches on it."

Pam watched another policeman sort through scraps of paper which he pulled from a wastebasket in the room. He examined each piece very carefully but apparently there was nothing which the intruder had left behind to reveal his identity. Pam walked over to observe him, and glanced down into the wastebasket. In one corner she spied a small, bent, black piece of wire which the officer had overlooked. Pam picked it up. It was a fishhook.

"Look, officer, this may be a clue," she said.

The policeman was astonished to find a bit of evidence that he had overlooked. He thanked Pam and carried the hook over to the others. "The little girl has found this fishhook, Sergeant," he said. "Maybe it was used to pick the lock on the case."

His superior took the hook and matched the point to the scratches. "You're right," he said.

"Maybe a fisherman was the thief," Pam suggested.

"That may be so," the sergeant replied, "but there're a lot of fishermen in Crestwood."

By this time Sergeant Costello was friendly to the children and when Pete asked him to describe the missing collection, he readily did so.

The coins had been in a black velvet-lined case, a photograph of which had appeared in the local newspaper. The officer also supplied the youngsters

"This fishhook may be a clue."

with a list of the stolen coins. "Are you going to play detective and find them for us?" he asked.

"We've solved other mysteries," Pete said. "We may be lucky on this case, too."

The sergeant praised Pam again for finding the fishhook, and the children left the museum.

"I wish you luck on your case, Detective Pam," Teddy remarked as they descended the steps to the sidewalk. "But how are you going to find the right fisherman?"

Pam pondered the question for a moment as they walked along. Then she said, "I think someone who plans to rob a place would first want to watch it for a while." She looked around. "What better spot to observe the museum from than that diner over there?" She pointed to a popular, shiny white eating-place diagonally across the town green from the museum.

Pete liked his sister's idea. "A person sitting next to a window in the diner could see when the custodian left at lunch time, and then walk into the place," he agreed.

As the four young detectives walked toward the diner, Teddy said, "Now we have *two* mysteries to solve—the one about the Oak Tree shilling and the theft of the collection."

"Can you think of a better way to spend a vacation?" Pete said with a chuckle and led the way into the restaurant.

Inside, a man wearing a white apron and cap was

wiping the counter with long, swift strokes. He glanced up and Pete said, "Did you notice any fisherman who ate here today?"

The counterman stopped, frowned and looked puzzled. "A fisherman? How could I tell a fisherman from anyone else?"

Pete suggested that his clothes might have been rough, or that he wore fishhooks in his hatband.

"No, I haven't seen anyone like that," the man replied.

Just then, someone from a booth called out, "Hello, Hollisters! Did you meet the rest of your tribe?"

They turned to see Dusty sipping a cup of coffee, and walked over to him. "What do you mean, Dusty?" Jean asked the jolly driver.

"I thought you knew," he said. "Ricky, Holly and Leo were my passengers not long ago."

Pete and Pam were surprised. "You let a dog ride the bus?" the girl asked him.

"Sure, why not? Leo thinks he's a person," Dusty replied, "so it's all right with me."

"But what are they doing in town?" Pete wanted to know.

Dusty shrugged. "I thought maybe they were looking for you."

"There's something wrong here," Pam whispered to her brother. "I'm going to phone Aunt Marge and find out."

She went into a telephone booth at the end of the

diner and dialed the number. She returned a few minutes later with an agitated look on her face. Aunt Marge reported that the young ones had left the house after getting a telephone call from Oz Brill. She didn't know where they had gone.

"Oh, Joey's up to something, I'll bet!" Pete declared. "Come on, let's look for those kids."

Leaving the diner they glanced about the town square. "There they are!" exclaimed Jean, pointing. Standing next to the fountain were Holly and Leo. The pig-tailed girl had Ricky's shoes and socks in her hands.

"Hello, Holly!" Pam cried as they ran up to the little girl. "What are you doing in town?"

Suddenly they noticed Ricky. He was wading in the pool on the other side of the fountain. Pam rushed up to him and called, "Ricky, get out of there! Wading's not allowed."

The red-haired boy explained that he had thrown a dime into the fountain by mistake, thinking it was a penny. "There it is," he said, looking down, and picked up the money.

"You get out of there this minute," his older sister chided him.

Ricky stepped out, shook one foot at a time, and sat down on the edge to put on his shoes and socks.

"We had a telephone call from Oz," Holly said innocently.

"What did he want?" Pete asked.

"He wanted to see us exactly at one-thirty," Ricky said, "in an alley beside the movie."

Pete glanced at his watch. It was not one-thirty yet. "I think it's some sort of a trick," he said. "Although I don't think Oz would do it all by himself. Joey's probably back of it."

After his shoes were on, Ricky stood up and looked around. "Say, where's Leo?" he exclaimed.

The cousins looked about for the shaggy Saint Bernard dog. He was not in sight.

"Oh, we've lost Leo!" Holly wailed.

CHAPTER 11

A *STARTLING DISCOVERY*

"Leo! Here, Leo!" Jean called out, as the children looked all about for the missing pet.

"Where could he have gone?" Teddy asked.

"He's such a big dog we should be able to see him," Pam declared. "I hope he hasn't been stolen!"

Pete suggested that they scatter in all directions in the search for the Saint Bernard dog. "We'll meet in front of the diner in five minutes. If we haven't found Leo by then, we can notify the police," he said.

They set out in twos; Teddy and Jean, Pete and Ricky, and Holly and Pam. They all searched behind parked cars and bushes in the town square, even in back of small shops facing on the street, but there was no sign of Leo. They questioned passersby, but no one could recall seeing the shaggy dog.

At last the six disappointed children met in front of the white diner. Holly and Ricky, especially, were crestfallen because they had brought the dog to town.

Pete suggested that perhaps some motorist had lured the dog into his car and had driven off with him. "We'll just have to ask the police to help us now," the boy said.

As he spoke, Dusty came out of the diner, "Why

so sad?" he said, noticing their long faces. "You look as if you've lost your best friend."

"We have," Jean said, her eyes filling with tears. "Leo is gone!"

"Don't worry, that old slowpoke couldn't have gone far," Dusty replied, trying to encourage them.

Just then he glanced at his bus, which he had left parked beside the curb halfway down the street.

"Were you children in my bus?" he asked.

"No," Pam said.

"Well, the door's open. I left it closed."

Dusty hurried to the parked vehicle, with the children at his heels.

"Well, the nerve of some customers!" the driver said as he stood with hands on hips looking into his bus.

"Leo! It's Leo!" Holly exclaimed. "Look, he's sitting in a seat."

They all climbed inside the bus to see the big dog seated like a regular passenger, waiting for the bus to go.

"He even looks impatient," Jean said as she threw her arms around the furry animal.

Leo went "Woof woof," and they all laughed.

"He pushed the door open," Dusty said. "But he's still going to have to pay his fare. Leo, fork it up. That'll be twenty-five cents."

Teddy held up the dog's right paw and the bus driver pretended to collect his fare. "Thank you, that's better," Dusty said.

"But we're not going to ride back now," Ricky objected.

"All right," Dusty said with a chuckle. "He's paid up for his next trip."

The cousins skipped out of the bus, with Leo following.

"It's almost time to meet Oz beside the movie," Pete said. "Let's hurry."

A few minutes later they trooped beneath the marquee of the theater, and as they approached the alley, Pete said, "Stop here while I take a peek. If this is Joey Brill's trap, we'll be ready for it."

Pete flattened himself against the side of the theater and peered around the corner. The alley was vacant except for Oz Brill, who stood beside his bicycle, looking very dejected. Pete motioned the others to follow him, and walked to where the boy was standing.

"Hi, Pete," Oz said, and brightened when he saw all the Hollisters. "Gee whiz, I'm glad to see you."

"What's the matter?" Pete asked. "Is Joey up to some trick?"

Briefly Oz said that he was having a miserable time with Joey visiting at his home. The older boy had bullied him and punched him whenever he could.

"Why does he do that?" asked Jean, looking very sympathetically at the thin boy.

"'Cause I told him I liked you Hollisters," Oz declared. "He twisted my arm and made me take back what I said."

"Well, what do you want us to do?" Teddy asked.

"I don't know," Oz replied, casting his eyes downward. "But can't you make him let me alone?"

"I wish we could send him back to Shoreham for you," Pam declared and then she added quickly, "Did Joey hear you make the telephone call?"

Oz shook his head. "I telephoned from the public booth next to the museum."

"Oh, then you know about the robbery," Jean declared.

"Robbery? No, what about it?"

Pam quickly told what had happened, and added, "Did you see anybody suspicious leave the building when you were making the phone call, Oz?"

The boy thought for a moment, then said, "The only person I saw was a man with a big brown shopping bag. He hurried straight to an old model car, jumped in and drove off."

"Which way did he go?" Pete asked eagerly.

When Oz said that the man had gone in the direction of the Hollisters' farm, the children's faces flushed with excitement.

"Oh, Oz, this is a great clue!" Pete said. "That's the only road out of town to the west, isn't it, Ted?"

When his cousin confirmed this, Pete suggested that they ride the bus along the route and look for the old auto which Oz had described.

"What about me?" the thin boy said sadly. "What am I going to do?"

Jean thought for a moment. "I have a plan," she

said. "Supposing we invite you and Joey to visit us for a day's fun."

"That would be a keen idea," Pam said.

"And we can keep an eye on Joey all day if he comes," Teddy remarked.

Pam suggested that perhaps she could talk Joey into being nice to his smaller cousin.

The young boy's eyes brightened when he heard this. Jean told him that she would send him an invitation. Then Oz said good-by and pedaled off toward home in Glenco.

"Come on!" Pete said. "Let's get back to the bus. It'll be leaving pretty soon."

With Leo lumbering along behind them, the children dashed to the bus stop. Dusty had just started the vehicle, and would not have seen them had not Pete raced forward in a burst of speed and rapped on the door. The driver braked sharply and they all piled inside.

Half a dozen passengers were seated in the bus, including a sour-looking, middle-aged man. When he saw Leo take a seat, he called to the driver, "No dogs are allowed on buses!"

Dusty looked around innocently. "A dog?" he asked.

"Yes, that big beast sitting over there!" the man replied.

"Oh," Dusty said as the children listened excitedly. "Leo is different. He thinks he's a person."

Dusty had just started off.

"Hmmph," snorted the man. "Well, come on, drive along, I'm in a hurry."

Pete chose a seat directly behind the driver, and asked him if he would keep on the lookout for the old car which Oz had mentioned.

"You bet I will," the man replied with a wink. "I've been a bus driver too long. I'd like to play detective with you."

Dusty and the children looked right and left as they drove out of town and down the country road which led to the Hollisters' farm. About halfway there Pete suddenly cried, "Look, Dusty!" He pointed to a little side lane where fresh-looking tire tracks led to the edge of a stream a short distance off the road.

"That's worth investigating," Dusty said, and stopped the bus.

As the children got out, Holly called, "Let's go, Leo!" With a sigh, the big dog slid from his seat, ambled slowly to the door and flopped off the bus.

"Come on, driver!" the unpleasant passenger said sharply. "Get along now, I'm in a hurry."

Dusty looked at Pete and shrugged, "I'm sorry I can't wait for you. I have to go on."

"That's all right," Pete said. "Thanks a lot. We'll walk the rest of the way."

When the bus had left, the children followed the tire tracks to the edge of the stream. Leo lay down in the shade of a tree.

"This is an old fishing hole," Teddy said. "I remember Dad talking about it."

"And the thief might have been a fisherman!" Pam declared.

"Look," Pete pointed out, "there are two sets of tire tracks. The car came down to the stream, then backed up again to the road." He followed the marks. "Then it drove back toward town," he said when he rejoined the others.

"But what was the car here for? That's what I'd like to know," Teddy asked.

The children glanced all about. Cattails grew on either side of the brook and ten feet downstream a graceful willow tree arched far out over a deep swirling pool.

Ricky wandered down the bank. Suddenly he called back to the others, "Hey, look, there's something floating over there!"

The others came running as Ricky pointed to a piece of black cloth bobbing in the swirling stream. It was caught on the tip end of the willow branch which bent over into the water.

"That could be the coin case!" Pam cried out. "Remember it was lined with black velvet!"

"How'll we reach it?" Holly asked.

"The brook's too deep to wade," said Jean.

"I have an idea!" Pete broke in. "I'm going to climb out on that willow limb. From there I can reach down and grab the cloth."

Just then Jean spotted a piece of fisherman's line caught in a bush, and pulled a safety pin from her pocket. "Here, Pete," she said, tying the line to the pin. "You can use this to fish out the cloth. Then you won't have to get so near to the end of that branch."

"That's a good idea," Pete said. He took the pin-hook from her, then climbed out carefully over the swirling water.

"Easy does it, cousin!" Teddy called to him. "Don't go out too far. That limb looks rotten to me."

Pete inched himself over the center of the stream. Then, holding on tightly with both legs and one arm, he dangled the safety pin until it caught one edge of the wriggling black cloth. He gave the fishing line a jerk.

"I've got it!" Pete said exultantly, but his cry was followed by a sickening *crack* as the willow branch splintered.

CHAPTER 12

FOLLOW THE LEADER

THE willow branch cracked but did not break off entirely. Instead, it sagged slowly toward the water, with Pete hanging on for dear life. When the tip end of the branch dipped deep into the swirling stream the limb ceased its downward plunge, leaving Pete stranded.

Inches from his fingers, however, lay the black velvet cloth. While the others on shore shouted encouragement, he picked the dripping material from the water. Attached to the lining was the wooden coin case—empty.

"What shall I do now?" Pete thought to himself as he watched the water gurgle and churn beneath him. He could drop off into the stream and swim ashore, or he could try to wriggle back along the broken limb.

"You can climb back," Teddy called out. "Try it!"

Pete could not turn about on the branch, so he had to back up an inch at a time, being careful not to fall off and also not to lose the coin case.

His muscles ached and his legs and arms were cramped but still Pete would not give up. Finally he wriggled his way past the crack in the wood. Once on the solid part of the limb, Pete swung the case toward the shore and it landed near Pam's feet. Then the boy scrambled quickly back to safety.

"I'll bet I know what happened," Pam said, after Pete had leaped down onto the shore of the stream. "The fisherman must have driven in here, removed the coins from the case and tossed it into the stream."

"That's it!" Holly said. "The water would have carried it far away and nobody would ever have found it."

"Except," Jean put in, "that it got stuck." Pam squeezed the water out of the dangling cloth, Pete put the case under his arm, and they started their walk back toward the Hollister farm. When they arrived, Mrs. Hollister and Aunt Marge were relieved to see them.

"Ricky! Holly!" their mother said sternly. "You shouldn't run off that way without telling me where you're going."

"I'm sorry," Holly said, "but I didn't think we'd be so long."

"I'm mad at you!" declared Sue, stamping her foot. "I wanted to go too." Then she dimpled. "But, I'm glad I stayed home because Aunt Marge and I made cookies."

Pam told her mother that everything had worked out all right because they had found a clue to the coin theft.

"And we'd like Joey and Oz to visit us, too," Jean added.

Seeing the confused looks on the faces of the women, Pam recounted what had happened since they left the house that morning.

"Goodness!" Aunt Marge declared, "what an exciting time you've had. And of course, I'll invite Joey and Oz to spend a day with us."

When Pete learned that his father and Uncle Russ were in the cartoonist's studio, he hastened to the little building, and showed them the empty coin case.

"Good work," Mr. Hollister said. "I think you should notify the police of this immediately."

Pete telephoned to police headquarters in Crestwood, and Sergeant Costello said he would dispatch a man immediately to get the coin case.

"You've discovered more than we have so far," the officer said. "Keep up the good work."

Half an hour later a police car pulled into the driveway. One of Sergeant Costello's men took the still damp case back to Crestwood.

After supper that evening Aunt Marge telephoned to Mrs. Brill, inviting the two boys out the next day. Joey's aunt agreed and promised to drive over with Joey and Oz.

Before the family sat down to breakfast the next morning, Pam called Sue, who had not appeared.

"Here I am!" her voice came from outdoors. Pam stepped into the back yard to see her little sister riding on the back of Leo. The Saint Bernard plodded along, looking very sad-faced.

"He won't gallop!" declared Sue. "I want to play cowboys and Indians."

Pam quickly lifted the little girl off the weary dog, explaining that Leo was not a pony.

While they ate breakfast, the children made plans for the day.

"We have time for some detective work before Joey and Oz arrive," Pete said. "Pam, let's go over to the Spencer estate and ask Mr. Spencer about the Oak Tree shilling."

Teddy and Jean said this would be a good idea as they had chores to do around the farm.

"It's the first big estate down the road," Teddy said. "You can't miss it because there's a sign at the entrance."

Pete made sure that the coin was in his pocket before he and Pam set off down the road. As they walked along Dusty's bus passed them and he honked and waved, holding up two fingers in a V-for-Victory sign.

"He must have heard that we found the coin case," Pete said grinning.

Half a mile down the road they came to an estate bordered by a low stone fence. They entered a gate with a wrought-iron sign reading "Eric Spencer" and proceeded along a wide gravely driveway bordered by tall trees. At the end of it stood an old mansion with high white pillars, Southern Colonial style.

Mr. Spencer himself met them at the door. "Welcome, young detectives," he said. "I was just about

"He won't gallop," declared Sue.

to telephone your uncle's home and congratulate you on that wonderful sleuthing you did yesterday."

Pam blushed at the praise and Pete grinned broadly.

"And now what did you want to see me about?" Mr. Spencer asked as he ushered them into a high-ceilinged living room.

When the two children had seated themselves on a brocade-covered sofa, Pete produced the mysterious Oak Tree shilling and handed it to the man.

"Oh yes. The coin the policeman found on you yesterday," Mr. Spencer said. "Where did you get it?"

Pete told him about finding the box caught in the tree roots, and Pam went on, "The property once belonged to your father, so this coin is rightly yours."

With a wave of his hand, the man smiled and said, "You keep it. I have no use for it, and besides, perhaps you can solve the mystery."

"That's what we really came to see you about, Mr. Spencer," Pete said. "Can you tell us who might have buried the coin?"

Mr. Spencer sat back in his chair. He kept flipping the shilling and catching it, and his eyes had a faraway look as if he were recollecting things deep in the past.

"Father was an eccentric man in some ways," he said. "He used to hide things and bury valuables. As a matter of fact, an old deed to important property was so well hidden that nobody to this day has found it."

"A deed?" Pam asked.

"Yes, a legal document about the sale of some land," Mr. Spencer continued, "and I need it very badly, too! Now as far as this coin is concerned, it may have to do with a paper I found in my father's strongbox."

Mr. Spencer gave the shilling back to Pete and excused himself. He returned a few minutes later with a scrap of white paper yellowed around the edges.

"Yes, just as I thought," the man said, "this old memorandum left by my father mentions, and I quote, 'something of great value hidden in the treasure oak.'"

Pete and Pam tingled with excitement. "Oh, what can it be?" the girl cried out.

"And where is the treasure oak?" Pete asked wryly.

"I'm afraid that'll be like finding a needle in a haystack," Mr. Spencer remarked.

"But I'm sure we're getting somewhere!" Pam said eagerly. "Does the bird figure mean anything to you, Mr. Spencer?"

The man pondered, then shook his head. "I'm afraid this is one of my father's mysteries that never will be solved."

As the host escorted his callers through the spacious hall to the front door, Pete noticed a large map hanging on the wall. It was covered by glass and bordered by an ornate frame. When the boy hesitated a moment to look at it, the man explained that it was an old map of the area.

"My father prized it," their host explained, "probably because it reminded him of his boyhood days, when Crestwood was a small country town."

Suddenly an idea occurred to Pete. Perhaps the old map might supply some clue to the whereabouts of the treasure oak! When he told Mr. Spencer this, the man chuckled. "I never saw youngsters so interested in sleuthing. If you'd like to study the map, I'll gladly lend it to you, provided you're very careful of it."

When Pete and Pam promised to take good care of the old relic, Mr. Spencer lifted it from the wall and gave it to them.

"Oh, Pete, that was a great idea," Pam said as soon as they were outside. The children retraced their steps along the broad driveway and turned down the road toward their cousins' farm.

Pete, who carried the map, could not keep from taking a peek at it now and then, but some of the lettering was so small that he could not make it out in the glinting sunlight.

"We'll use the magnifying glass when we get back," Pam said as they hastened along the side of the road.

The Hollister family was sitting down for lunch by the time they arrived. Pete carefully put the map on his bed, and joined the others at the table.

"Joey and Oz haven't arrived yet," Mrs. Hollister said, "but I expect they'll come after lunch." She told the children that she and her husband and Aunt Marge were going to town. Uncle Russ had work to do in his studio, so the cousins would have to entertain Joey and Oz alone.

"Mind you, now," Aunt Marge cautioned, "no trouble!"

Pam thought that Joey would be so interested in the farm, that he would forget his mischief. "And we'll take good care of Oz," she promised.

After the adults had left, Pete and Pam brought the old map into the living room to show Teddy and Jean. Pam took out the magnifying glass and they were all about to study it when a car drove up.

Pam hastened to the window and said, "It's Mrs. Brill with Joey and Oz."

The cousins ran outdoors to welcome their guests. "Thank you so much for inviting the two boys," Mrs. Brill said. "I'll call for them later. Now, be good," she said, "and have fun!"

No sooner had Joey's aunt disappeared when he spied the dogcart sitting in front of the barn. At the same time Leo trotted up and licked Oz's hand.

"He recognizes me," the thin boy said happily.

"When did you see that dog before?" Joey asked with a look of suspicion in his eyes. But the others said nothing about their meeting in town.

"Leo's friendly to everybody," Jean remarked.

"Well, the first thing I want is a ride in that dog-cart," Joey said.

"You're pretty large," Pete declared.

"Sure, I'm the heaviest of anybody," Joey boasted. He dragged Leo by the collar and harnessed him, then stood up in the cart. "I'm a Roman chariot driver," he said. "Come on, giddap!"

Leo did not budge. He stood in the traces, turned his head and looked at Joey very sadly.

"Come on, you stupid dog!" the boy shouted. "Give me a ride!"

When Leo still would not move, Joey jumped out of the cart and picked up a stick.

"Don't you dare hit him!" Pam cried.

Pete said nothing but he gave Joey a look that made the bully realize he would tolerate no nonsense.

"Okay," Joey said. "Let's play a game then. How about follow-the-leader? I'll be the leader!"

"All right," Pete said. Everybody liked the idea, even little Sue, who insisted on playing the game, too. Pam took her by the hand and Joey raced off. He ran around the barn, dashed out into the field, and jumped over a small fence. The others followed close behind. Oz had trouble keeping up and Pete waited for the smaller boy while Ricky and Holly trailed close on Joey's heels.

"Ha, I can do everything better than anybody!" Joey cried as he shinned up a small tree, swung out on a low branch and dropped to the ground. He was now far ahead of the others. He raced into the barn, and when Ricky and Holly dashed through the door they could not see him.

"He must have run off into that field with the tall grass," Holly said and hurried out again.

When Pam and Sue came into the barn, Joey suddenly jumped up from behind a bale of hay, where he had been hiding, and blocked the door.

"Let us out of here," Pam said.

Joey pushed her to the floor and dashed out, swinging the big door closed. Pam and Sue heard him bolt it.

"Now, I'm going to get that lazy dog!" Joey threatened.

CHAPTER 13

BALD EAGLE HILL

"Joey, don't you dare hit Leo!" Pam called out. She flung herself against the closed barn door, but it was securely locked from the outside. Then she banged on it with her fists. The only response was Joey's laughter.

"Here, Leo, come here," she heard him say in a mock friendly voice.

"If I could only call for help," Pam thought. She glanced up at a loft over her head. Stairs led up to it and at the head of the flight was a large window. Pam and Sue climbed the steps. The older girl tugged at the window, but it would not budge. Outside she saw Joey Brill, with a stick held behind his back, approaching the unsuspecting Saint Bernard.

"Oh Joey, don't do it!" Pam shouted again.

The bully turned to look up at the window. Seeing the faces of the two girls, he brandished the stick at them. But at that moment, Leo stood up on his hind legs and placed his two big furry paws squarely on Joey's shoulders.

"Ow, get down!" Joey exclaimed, stepping backward.

Leo moved right along with the boy and licked his face.

"Oof, get away, you big beast!" the bully cried.

The expressions on the faces of the two girls changed from fear to laughter. Sue giggled, and said, "They're dancing together, how nice!"

Joey, meanwhile, could not shake off Leo. The dog's paws rested so heavily upon his shoulders that he was unable to swing his stick. Turning his head, Joey saw the girls laughing at him. Flustered, he tripped and fell over backwards.

Just then Pete ran up, followed by the others who were playing follow-the-leader. Pete howled when he saw the funny scene. "You win, Joey, nobody else could do what you just did!"

The bully scrambled to his feet, his face red. Pam meanwhile ran down from the loft and banged on the barn door. Teddy heard her and opened it, but Joey did not wait to be accused. He dashed off across a field and into the woods, while Pam told her story.

"It serves him right," Jean remarked after hearing about the bully's mean trick.

"The worst thing you can do to Joey is laugh at him," Pete said. "Well, that gets rid of him for a little while. Now we can have some fun."

Although Oz said nothing, he looked very pleased to be alone with the Hollister children.

"Come on," Jean said. "Let's go down to the basement playroom."

All except Pete and Teddy clattered down the outside steps and entered a large bright rumpus room. In it was a Ping-pong table, a phonograph with records, and off to one side, a desk with piles of paper and crayons.

"Oh, may I draw a picture?" Oz asked.

"Of course, if you'd like to," Jean replied pleasantly.

Oz said that he loved to draw. Then, as the others watched with admiration, the boy quickly made a sketch of Pam.

"Oh, that's great!" Ricky declared. "Will you draw a picture of me, too?"

While Oz was having fun sketching his playmates, Pete and Teddy went into the living room, took the magnifying glass and studied the glass-covered map, hoping to find a clue.

"Crickets!" Pete said, as his finger followed the main road through Crestwood. "Look, there were hardly any side streets in those days."

The place where the Hollisters' farm now stood was vacant land. The Spencer estate was clearly indicated, with boundaries stretching to the edge of the map. There, Pete noticed some small printing nearly hidden by the edge of the picture frame. The boy held a magnifying glass over the tiny letters. They spelled out "Bald Eagle Hill."

"Do you suppose that was on the old estate, Teddy?" Pete asked.

"It looks like it."

"Say!" Pete declared, snapping his fingers. "You remember the bird on the old coin? Could that represent a bald eagle?"

Quickly the boys studied the coin again under the magnifying glass. "It *could* be a bald eagle," Teddy said.

"Are there any oak trees growing on Bald Eagle Hill?" was Pete's next question.

"I've never been there," Teddy said. "Let's ask Dad!"

With Pete carrying the framed map, the two boys hurried out toward Uncle Russ's studio. As they passed the corner of the house, a voice called out, "Where are you guys going?"

The cousins hesitated and turned to see Joey Brill. His arm was cocked and in his hand he held a large rock.

"Don't throw it!" Pete warned him.

"You can't laugh at me and get away with it!" the bully cried.

Pete and Teddy dashed for the cartoonist's studio. The stone flew from Joey's hand and arched through the air.

"Look out, Pete!" Teddy yelled, but too late. The rock landed squarely in the middle of the map, shattering the glass into a hundred pieces.

"Now you've done it, Joey Brill!" Pete cried out angrily. "This is very valuable and it doesn't belong to us."

"See if I care," Joey sneered, just as Uncle Russ stepped from his studio.

"What's all the noise about?" the cartoonist asked,

"Look out, Pete!" Teddy yelled.

surveying the jagged bits of glass scattered at Pete's feet.

When told what had happened, Uncle Russ ordered Joey to come over and pick up the debris.

"I won't have any stone-throwing on this farm," the man said sternly. "If you cause any more trouble before your aunt arrives, I'll take you home in my car. Now get a broom and dustpan out of the barn and clean up this mess!"

As Joey obeyed, Teddy explained that the old map belonged to Mr. Spencer. "Come with me, boys," his father said. "I have some glass and glazing tools in the studio. We can make this as good as new again."

While his uncle looked for a piece of glass the right size, Pete queried him about oak trees on Bald Eagle Hill.

"I can't say that I remember any growing there," Uncle Russ replied. "But I haven't been on Spencer's place for years."

The man carefully placed the framed map on his tidy workbench. Then with a fine chisel he began to pry the back off the old frame, so he could insert the new glass.

As the last tiny nail came loose, the backing slid off. Directly beneath it was a piece of cardboard. Pete lifted it out.

Much to everybody's surprise, an official-looking document lay between the cardboard and the map.

"What's this?" Uncle Russ asked, as he pulled out the stiff piece of paper.

A prickling sensation started on the back of Pete's neck and worked up to his scalp. "Uncle Russ!" he blurted. "Does that look like a deed?"

His uncle studied the document carefully. "I believe it is one, Pete. Something to do with the Spencer property."

Teddy let out a war whoop. "Maybe this is the missing deed you told us about, Pete!"

"Don't put it back, Uncle Russ," his nephew said. "Mr. Spencer will want to see this."

The boys could hardly wait until the cartoonist repaired the glass and replaced the back of the old frame.

"Come on, Teddy!" Pete said. "Let's hop over to Mr. Spencer's right away."

Smiling at their eagerness, Uncle Russ offered to drive the boys to the old estate. After telling the children in the playroom where they were going, the boys hopped into the waiting car. When Uncle Russ let them off at the front door of the mansion he said he would wait and take them home.

The boys hurried up the stairs, with Teddy carrying the framed map and Pete holding the deed. This time Mr. Spencer's maid met them at the door. When Pete introduced Teddy and himself and asked for Mr. Spencer she said, "I don't think he can see you now."

"But he must—I mean, please, may we see him? It's important!" Pete said.

"All right," the woman replied reluctantly, "I'll tell him."

"Crickets!" Pete whispered to his cousin. "We have to see him now. This is a hot clue!"

The maid appeared moments later and ushered the boys into a comfortable study, where Mr. Spencer was seated behind a large mahogany desk.

"Hello, boys," he said. "Have you found a clue to the old coin?"

"More than that!" Pete burst out. "Look at this!" He stepped over and placed the document on the desk. Mr. Spencer looked at it in astonishment. "This—this is the missing deed! Where did you find it?"

When Pete told his story, the man shook his head slowly, and said, "To think it's been in my own home all these years, right under my very nose!"

"You boys don't know what this means to me," he continued. "My claim to Bald Eagle Hill was always in doubt. Now I know for sure that the property belongs to me."

The boys looked at each other wide-eyed.

"Bald Eagle Hill!" Pete said. "Are there any oak trees growing there?"

Mr. Spencer turned to a large picture window behind his desk and pointed to a rolling hill about a mile distant. "Bald Eagle Hill is crowned with very old oak trees," he said.

Teddy pulled at his cousin's arm. "Pete!" he exclaimed. "We've solved it!"

CHAPTER 14

A TELLTALE SKETCH

"Not so fast, Teddy!" Pete cautioned. "We don't even know what the treasure is yet."

"Besides there are dozens of oaks on that hill," Mr. Spencer said, and added, "if you wish to scout around up there, take the private road at the back of the house. It stops at the foot of Bald Eagle Hill. You can hike up the rest of the way. If you see Rogers, my caretaker, tell him I gave you permission to explore there."

After thanking Mr. Spencer, the cousins left to join Uncle Russ, who was waiting in the car.

"You may unravel this mystery yet!" he exclaimed when they told him what Mr. Spencer had said. "And if you do, I'm going to use the story for my next comic strip!"

The three drove around the house and down a winding dirt road. Soon the fields on the estate gave way to thick woods, and by the time the road ended, they found themselves in a forest of oaks and pines.

Uncle Russ parked the car and the three set off on foot up the steep slope toward the top of Bald Eagle Hill. Although the sun shone hot overhead, the woods were cool and the boys drew in great gulps of sweet fresh air as they threaded their way among the trees.

"Here's the top of the hill!" Pete said, running on ahead with Teddy. They broke into a circular clearing. All about it stood towering oaks, several of which had been uprooted or tilted by the twister. There was no sign of the caretaker.

"What a grand view," Uncle Russ said as he shaded his eyes and gazed across to an expanse of land on the other side of the hill. "There's the Crestwood Golf Course," he said. "I've played there several times."

Then he turned to Pete and Teddy. "Well, boys," he said, "which one is the treasure oak?"

Teddy sat down on a log and scratched his head. "The mystery is still far from solved," he said sadly.

Pete glanced about at the sturdy tree trunks, and sighed, "I guess we'll have to examine every tree here."

"Even that wouldn't prove anything," his uncle replied. "Unless you X-ray them all."

Pete suggested that perhaps Mr. Turner might be able to help with the problem, and they started back toward the car. Halfway down the hill, a huge buck deer dashed from a thicket and ran across their path. "Crickets, that gave me a fright!" Pete said with a laugh.

"And speaking of frights," Teddy said, "I wonder how they're making out with Joey back on the farm."

Fortunately for the rest of the children, Uncle

Russ's scolding of Joey Brill had had a good effect, for the bully did not disturb the youngsters at their drawing in the basement recreation room.

The Hollister cousins grew more excited by the minute as Oz displayed an unusual skill. The pictures he had drawn of Ricky, Pam, Holly and Sue were so good that they could not wait to tell Uncle Russ about it.

"Someday you may be a famous cartoonist like Daddy," Jean said and the boy beamed with delight.

Then an idea struck Pam. "Oz!" she exclaimed. "Can you draw from memory?"

"Yes, sometimes."

"Could you draw a picture of that man you saw leaving the museum when the coins were stolen?"

"I think I can," he said, as Pam handed him a fresh sheet of drawing paper.

Oz hunched his slender shoulders over the table and, thinking carefully, drew a picture of a man's face. When he had finished, Pam gasped in amazement. "That's the man I saw near the fountain on Sunday!"

"The one you thought was looking for something?" Jean asked.

"Yes!" Pam declared. "Oh, Oz, you've given us a wonderful clue! Let's tell Uncle Russ and the boys. I think I hear the car."

As Pam and Jean raced up the basement stairs, the cartoonist drove into the farm. The girls ran toward the car waving a piece of paper. Even before

"That's the man!" Pam exclaimed.

Pete, Teddy and Uncle Russ could get out, Jean shouted, "We know who stole the coins from the museum! Look, here's his picture!"

"My, that's a fine sketch," her father said. "Who did it?"

"Oz!" the girls chorused.

"But who is this man?"

"We don't know his name, Uncle Russ," Pam said, "but I saw him lurking by the fountain in front of the Town Hall."

Once they were inside the living room, excitement over the two mysteries ran higher than ever. After stories were exchanged, Jean showed her father more of Oz's drawings.

"This boy has a fine style," Uncle Russ said, putting an arm around Oz Brill. "You have real talent."

The boy looked pleased. "But I wish I could be a detective like Pete and Pam," he said shyly.

"What are you going to do next about your cases?" Uncle Russ asked the children.

"Maybe we should take Oz's drawing of the suspect to the police," Pete said, "so they can start looking for the man."

"But we're not positive he is the thief," Pam pointed out. "It wouldn't be fair to have him arrested now. Let's see if we can find the man first and question him. We'll see if he acts guilty."

Pete agreed. "If he does, we can tell the police then."

"First thing in the morning," Pam went on,

"we'll post lookouts at the fountain in case the man comes there again."

"While the rest of you do that," Pete added, "I'll visit Mr. Turner to see if he can help us discover which tree is the treasure oak."

Uncle Russ nodded. "Excellent planning. That way you will cover both your mysteries."

As he spoke, there was the sound of cars in the driveway. Aunt Marge arrived with Mr. and Mrs. Hollister and directly behind them came Mrs. Brill for her nephew and Oz. Joey was nowhere in sight, but when his aunt called, he appeared at the edge of the woods.

"Did you have any trouble with him today?" Mrs. Brill asked as Joey sauntered across the field toward her car.

"Hardly any," Uncle Russ replied generously. "I think that boy needs to romp in the woods and burn off his excess energy."

Joey seemed relieved when nothing more was said. Then he and Oz got into the car.

"I've had the most wonderful time, Mother!" Oz said excitedly. "Pete has almost solved the mystery of the Oak Tree shilling! Mr. Turner, the tree man, is going to help him tomorrow!"

"Come back again sometime, Oz," Jean said. "And maybe Daddy can give you some lessons in drawing cartoons." The thin boy looked very pleased as they drove off.

At dinner that evening the excited cousins recounted the day's events. When Uncle Russ carved a large roast chicken, Sue declared that she felt sorry for a bald eagle.

"Gracious, why is that?" her mother asked. "Wouldn't you like to fly high up in the sky like an eagle?"

"But bald eagles have no feathers," Sue came back. "They must look like this chicken."

Everybody giggled and Pam explained to her little sister that the bald eagle got its name from the white patch on its head.

"Oh, that's better," Sue said with a relieved sigh.

"Pete," his father remarked, "you have only a few more days to solve these mysteries. We'll be going home soon."

"Yikes!" Ricky said, "Daddy, we can't go home until everything's been cleared up!"

"Goody!" Holly said as she passed her plate for a second helping of white meat. "That means we'll be here for a long time."

"Tomorrow will be another day of sleuthing," Pete said and told his parents of their plans. Mr. and Mrs. Hollister agreed, but added that they would like Holly and Sue to remain at home with Leo. The girls readily agreed, especially when Aunt Marge promised to let them help her bake apple pies.

When Dusty passed with his bus next morning he found the cousins eagerly waiting to be picked up.

"Hop in, all of you," he said, swinging open the bus door. "Special bargain rates today. Instead of twenty-five cents, it's two bits."

"You wouldn't like it if I bit you twice," Jean said with a smile.

"Just for that," the bus driver remarked with a wink at the other children, "I'll charge you a double half fare."

Dusty put the bus in gear. It lurched and groaned, then started once more in the direction of Crestwood. The driver peered at his passengers in the rearview mirror and asked, "Where's the rest of the tribe?"

"They're home baking apple pies," Pam replied.

"Oh, that Leo! He can do anything."

The children giggled. When they arrived at the town square, Dusty let his young passengers off.

"Don't forget to bring me a piece of Leo's apple pie," he called cheerfully.

The youngsters waved good-by, then began the serious business of a detective stakeout. It was agreed that Pam, Jean, and Teddy should station themselves at vantage points near the fountain to watch for the coin thief. Pete and Rick, meanwhile would visit Mr. Turner in the Town Hall.

The two boys hurried off, ran down the steps to the basement office and hastened to Mr. Turner's desk.

"Good morning," the man said cheerfully. "How are the young detectives doing today?"

"We need your help, Mr. Turner," Pete said, and told about the clues which had led them to Bald Eagle Hill.

"If something is hidden in one of those trees," the forester said, "it's going to be very hard to find it."

The tree man explained that any hole or cut made in a tree would heal over, leaving a scar. "But a broken branch would leave the same kind of a mark."

"In other words," Pete said, "you wouldn't know from the scar whether it was made by accident or on purpose."

"I'm afraid that's right," Mr. Turner said. "It'll be some job to examine all the marks on those old oak trees."

"That could take months," Ricky said with a sigh.

"Right! And even then you might never find the treasure," the tree man added. Suddenly his eyes brightened, "Let's see that coin again, Pete."

When the boy handed it to him, Mr. Turner studied the old piece intently. "It could be," he said, "that the branches of the treasure tree are shaped much the same as the ones on this coin."

"Crickets, I never thought of that!" Pete exclaimed. "Thank you, Mr. Turner."

"But there you have a problem, too," the man said. "With the trees in full leaf, it will be hard to see the branches."

"We'll try anyway," Pete declared.

"Tell you what," the tree man said, "I'll see if I can help you boys."

"When?" asked Ricky.

"I'll pick you up at ten o'clock tomorrow morning," Mr. Turner promised.

"That'll be great!" Pete declared and both boys thanked the forester. Then the pair hurried over to the fountain to help the girls. As they approached the long plumes of spouting water, they could see Pam and Jean peeking out from behind trees. Teddy was crouched behind a low bench.

Pam saw her brothers coming, and at almost the same time, noticed a man walking toward the fountain. Her heart fluttered. He was the man she had seen there on Sunday—the one Oz had drawn. She was certain he was the thief.

The man hastened to the wishing pool, bent over and looked anxiously into it. As he did, Pam signaled the others and they approached the stranger.

Seeing them, he started to leave but Pam walked up to him. "Do you know what happened to the lost coins?" she asked.

The stranger's eyes widened in a startled look as he saw the ring of children closing around him. Without a word, he pushed roughly between Pete and Ricky and started to run.

"Stop, thief! Stop!" Pam cried out. The man made a beeline for a rickety old car parked at the curb and all the children set off in hot pursuit. In a burst of speed, Pete and Teddy caught up with the stranger and grabbed his arms while Ricky made a flying leap at the back of his belt.

"Help, police!" Jean screamed.

CHAPTER 15

FLYING KITTENS

THE man struggled and thrashed about until a policeman on traffic duty nearby ran to investigate the commotion.

"What's all this fighting about?" he asked, as the boys released the captive.

"We think this is the fellow who stole the coin collection from the museum," Pete said.

"I didn't do it," the man protested. "These kids have mistaken me for someone else."

"What's your name?" the officer asked the man, whose hands now were shaking.

"Kip Lucas. Everybody knows me," he added. "I'm a handyman. I've worked all over Crestwood."

"Are you the one they call 'Fishy Lucas?'"

"Yes."

"Quite a fisherman, I understand," the policeman said.

"And we found the coin case in an old fishing hole along the stream," Teddy said. "He's the thief, all right, officer."

The policeman did not know whom to believe. But just to make certain, he marched Kip Lucas to Police Headquarters located in the rear of the Town

Hall. The children followed, amid stares of passersby who wanted to know what the trouble was.

Inside the police station, Sergeant Costello was at the desk.

"Hi, detectives!" he called, seeing the Hollisters. Then his eyebrows raised when he observed Fishy Lucas and the policeman.

"I think we've caught the coin thief," Pete declared.

Again the prisoner denied having anything to do with the missing collection. Quickly Pam produced Oz's sketch from the pocket of her blouse, explained where the young artist had seen the man. When she told of the thief's old getaway car Lucas's knees seemed to sag.

"You'd better tell the truth, Fishy," the sergeant warned. He added, "I notice you haven't been working lately. Just spending your time fishing."

The officer told the Hollisters that Lucas was a handyman, who had formerly been a locksmith.

"That's how he opened the display case with a fishhook!" Ricky guessed.

Lucas hung his head and half whispered, "So you found the fishhook, too. All right, I took the coins, but they were mine!"

"Yours?" the sergeant said in a loud voice. "What gives you that idea?"

Fishy Lucas, appearing sad and dejected, told a story which surprised the children. He said that he was the son of Silas Lucas, who had been a servant of old Mr. Spencer's.

"My father worked for him long and faithfully," the prisoner said, "and old Mr. Spencer promised to leave some valuable coins to him."

"Didn't he get them?" asked Pam sympathetically.

"No! They were left to the museum just before my father died."

"How do we know what you're saying is the truth?" the policeman demanded.

"I have proof," came the reply. Fishy took out his wallet, thumbed through some papers and produced an old letter, so worn that it almost fell apart. He spread it on the sergeant's desk. Pete and Pam peered over the officer's shoulders to read the note.

Written in ink, it was signed by Eli Spencer and promised six valuable coins to Silas Lucas. Pete read the list aloud. "One New England shilling, one Willow Tree sixpence, one 1796 Half dollar and three Silver dollars, 1794, 1797 and 1836. Crickets! Those are good ones! They're worth lots of money!"

"It looks as if your father was promised some coins," Sergeant Costello admitted.

"But maybe they're not the ones which were left to the museum," Teddy ventured.

"We can find out," Pam said. "Do you have the list of stolen coins, Pete?"

"Right here," her brother replied and took from his pocket the typewritten sheet given to him by Sergeant Costello on the day of the theft.

"No need for me to get my copy out then," the officer said with a twinkle in his eye. He and the two children scanned the names of the stolen coins. Not one was included in the old list which Fishy had produced.

"So you see," the officer said sternly, "the coins you stole did not belong to your father or to you. Now give them back."

Fishy glared at the children, then stared at the floor, but did not reply.

"If you don't, we'll have to search your house," the officer said.

He removed a set of handcuffs from his belt and was about to snap them on the wrists of the prisoner when Pam intervened. "Oh please, don't do that," she said. "Mr. Lucas won't run away, will you?"

Kip Lucas looked glum. Then he shook his head slowly and said, "Run away? Where would I go?"

"All right," the sergeant agreed. "You're a kind girl, Pam. If Fishy will tell where he hid the coins, I think we might even let him go, despite his mistaken idea of who owned the museum pieces.

"Jackson," he said to the arresting officer, "we'll take everyone out to Fishy's place. I'm sure we'll find the coins there." The sergeant led the group out to the police cars parked at the curb.

"Yikes!" Ricky cried out. "Riding in a police car will be fun!"

Sergeant Costello, Fishy and the two older boys rode together while Policeman Jackson took the other children in the second car. They drove in the direction of Glenco, then turned off on a side road, and stopped before a tiny shack.

"You youngsters stay here," the sergeant instructed them, "while Jackson and I take Fishy inside and search his place."

Fifteen minutes later, the police returned, shaking their heads. "We didn't find anything," Officer Jackson declared.

Before they got back into the car, Sergeant Costello looked sternly at the prisoner. "You'd better tell us where you hid those coins, because I'm going to keep you in a cell until you do."

"Oh dear!" Pam said. "Please tell him, Mr. Lucas. I don't want to see you go to jail." But despite the girl's plea, Fishy Lucas remained stonily silent.

"Okay, come along," the sergeant said and beckoned Fishy into his car.

Policeman Jackson was instructed to take the children home. Upon arriving at the farm, they dashed into the house to find the grownups chatting in the living room.

"You really found the thief?" Aunt Marge asked, hardly able to believe the thrilling story of the children's detective work.

"We sure did," Teddy said, proudly. "But Fishy will have to stay in jail until he confesses to where he hid the coins."

"That's too bad," Uncle Russ declared. "Fishy's really not a bad sort."

Both of the Hollister men recalled Silas Lucas. They remembered, too, that Fishy had been a shift-less sort of fellow, but never harmful.

"He just thinks that an injustice has been done to him," Pam said. "He's all mixed up. I do wish he'd tell."

As they finished their report, the cousins heard gleeful shouts coming from behind the house. They hastened out to see what kind of game Holly and Sue were playing.

"Oh, isn't that cute!" declared Pam, who was first to spy the younger children.

Holly and Sue were leading Leo, who was hitched to the dogcart. On the seat rode White Nose and her five kittens! A blue ribbon, tied to the mother cat's paws, stretched to Leo's collar.

But the big dog did not seem to be enjoying him-self. He stopped, whereupon Sue pulled a dog biscuit from her pocket and held it in front of his nose. Leo took it in one gulp, licked his chops and moved on again.

"That's a real slow-motion dog," Pete said, "if you don't mind my saying so."

But just then White Nose became impatient. The cat leaped off the seat right onto Leo's back, and clung to him with her sharp claws.

"Oh dear," Jean squealed as Leo yipped. The slow-motion dog took off like a giddy pup. The cart bounced this way and that, with the cats flying off in all directions. White Nose dashed up a small

Leo yipped and took off.

maple tree at the corner of the house. Her kittens followed as if by command.

Teddy and Jean ran after the frightened dog. They ruffled his furry coat, but could find no damage.

"I guess the cat only scared him," Jean said as they led Leo back to his kennel. Meanwhile, White Nose and her kittens perched on a long limb like birds on a telephone wire. The blue ribbon had pulled off Leo's collar and was now hanging limply around the mother cat's neck.

"Oh, those poor frightened little babies," Sue said, looking up into the tree.

"Never mind, I'll get them down," Pete offered. He went to the barn and returned with a ladder which he placed against the branch. Carefully, he rescued the kittens first. Then he perched White Nose on his shoulder and climbed down with her.

Holly twirled one of her pigtails, and tightened her mouth until her dimples showed. "Well, I guess cats and dogs don't mix," she said.

After lunch, Holly and Sue played with the kittens and did not bother Leo any more. Several times Pam telephoned police headquarters, only to learn that Fishy Lucas still kept his secret and would not talk about the missing coins.

At nightfall, the telephone rang. Pam answered. "Long distance for Pam Hollister," said the operator.

"This is she," replied the girl, surprised.

A muffled voice at the other end said, "I'm the

thief. The coins were thrown into the brook where the coin case was found." Then the caller hung up.

Pam told the others what had happened. "Could it have been Fishy?" she wondered.

Teddy called police headquarters. The handyman was still in jail and had not telephoned.

"The call was long distance," Pam said puzzled, "and nobody knows I'm here but our family and friends in Shoreham."

"Someone in Glenco knows," declared Pete wryly.

"Of course!" exclaimed Pam, catching on. "Joey Brill!"

"It would be just like him," Ricky said, disgusted.

"He's not fooling us this time," Pete said.

"But you can never tell what he might do," Pam reminded him. "We'll have to be careful."

That night when everyone was asleep, Holly wakened and roused Sue sleeping beside her. "Do you hear something?" she whispered to her little sister. Both girls listened. The noise came again.

"Somebody's moaning!" Holly said, and little Sue called out in fright, "Mother! Mother!"

CHAPTER 16

A HAPPY REPORT

MRS. Hollister, wrapped in her bathrobe, answered Sue's frantic call. "What's the matter, dear?" she asked, bending over the frightened little girl.

"There's an awful noise," Sue told her.

Mrs. Hollister listened. From Pam's room, across the hall, came the weird cry again. Mrs. Hollister hastened to Pam's door, flung it open, switched on the light and stepped inside. The little girls were close at her heels.

Pam stood at the foot of the bed. Her eyes were wide open. "Help! Help!" she cried feebly.

"She's still sleeping," Holly said. "Wake her up, Mother!"

Mrs. Hollister put her arms around Pam and rested the girl's fluffy blonde head on her shoulder.

"Wake up, Pam," Mrs. Hollister said gently. "You're having a nightmare. Everything's all right."

"Nobody bad is going to get you," Sue piped up, "'cause we're here, that's why!"

Pam began to cry softly, but with her mother comforting her, she soon dried her tears and looked sheepishly about her. "Oh, I'm sorry, Mother," she said. "That was such an awful dream."

By now sleepy-eyed Ricky and Pete, along with Mr. Hollister, stood in the doorway.

"Maybe Pam has a stomach ache," Ricky said.

"Are you sure of that, Doc?" his father asked with a wink.

"It was only a dream, Daddy," Pam told him. "In it Fishy was chasing me all around the fountain, because he had hidden the coins in the water and wanted to keep me away from them."

"Crickets!" Pete exclaimed. "That may be the right answer, Pam!"

"Yikes!" Ricky added. "Pam solves mysteries in her sleep!"

Mrs. Hollister said that this might not be as big a joke as it seemed and everyone sat down on the bed to discuss the strange dream.

"Maybe the first time Pam saw Fishy, he was looking for a place to hide the coins, even before he had stolen them," Pete suggested.

"And later, after he had hidden them in the fountain," Holly guessed, "he came back to see that they were not disturbed."

The questions and answers flew back and forth until the entire household had been aroused and gathered in Pam's room.

"There's only one thing to do," Mr. Hollister said finally, "and that's to search in the fountain."

"All right," his wife agreed. "Now off to bed, children. We can look for the coins in the morning."

"But, Mother," Pete protested, "let's do it now!"

"At three o'clock in the morning?"

"Maybe he has a point," Uncle Russ said. "It's quiet there now with no one to disturb us."

The idea of searching in the fountain's chilly waters in the middle of the night made the cousins wide awake with excitement.

"All right," Mrs. Hollister said. "Pete and Pam may go. But the rest of you Indians—off to bed!"

Aunt Marge agreed to let Teddy and Jean accompany their cousins to the fountain.

"How about me, too?" Mr. Hollister asked grinning. "I'll drive them to town."

The younger children looked disappointed, but when Pam promised to give them a full report, their faces brightened and they returned to bed.

The four cousins dressed quickly, armed themselves with flashlights, and hopped into Mr. Hollister's station wagon. They were soon on their way to Crestwood. How different the town looked in the middle of the night! The streets were empty and dark, and even the fountain stood silent.

"Crickets!" Pete said. "There's no water coming out of it."

Mr. Hollister explained that the fountain was shut off at midnight and turned on again at seven in the morning.

He parked the car and they got out. At the edge of the pool the children quickly stripped off their shoes and socks. As they stepped into the cold water they let out muffled squeals. They flashed their lights onto the rocky bottom. "Oo, the stones are slimy," Jean said as she walked gingerly.

"Careful—don't slip," Mr. Hollister cautioned them.

Bending their faces as close to the water as possible, the searchers walked round and round the fountain.

"Ow!" Pete yelped. He reached into the water and picked up a small tin boat which had sunk there.

"The coins are tickling my feet!" Pam giggled.

There were lots of nickels, dimes and pennies underfoot, but no sign of the coins they wanted.

"I don't imagine they were just thrown in loose," Mr. Hollister said.

Pete agreed. "They're probably in a box or a bag of some sort," he said and added with a sigh, "if they're here at all."

"Don't give up so easily," Pam scolded her brother.

"Who said I'm giving up?"

"Oh, we'll search until daylight," Teddy declared. "But when they start the fountain again, we'll get all wet."

Pam thought she saw a sack near the base of the fountain, but all she pulled up was a round stone. As she plopped it back into the water, the girl straightened up and sighed. "Maybe I didn't dream the right answer after all."

"Who's giving up now?" Pete asked. Pam grinned and quickly resumed her search.

After nearly an hour, Mr. Hollister glanced at his watch. "I'm afraid it's no use," he said. "We'd better go now."

"Just another few minutes, Daddy," Pam pleaded.

At that moment Jean stubbed her toe against a rock the size of a football. It moved. "Come here, Teddy, help me with this," she called to her brother.

The two children pulled the rock aside. The beams of their flashlights glistened through the water and came to rest on a milky-white object. Jean pulled it out of the water.

"It looks like a plastic cheese box or something," she said.

With a flick of his finger, Teddy flipped off the lid.

The box was full of old coins!

"Daddy, we've found it!" Pam exulted.

"Uncle John!" Jean cried out. "The dream was true! It was really true!"

The children stepped out of the water and sat on the rim surrounding the fountain. They took each coin and examined it carefully.

"These are the right ones!" Pete said. "I remember some of them from the list of the museum pieces."

"Get your shoes and socks on," Mr. Hollister said, "and we'll take these coins to headquarters."

Two dim blue lights burned on either side of the entrance to the police station. As the group marched along the silent marble corridor, their shoes sounded

"Daddy, we've found it!" Paul exulted.

like heavy boots. In a large room the night sergeant, a thin, gray-haired man, looked up from his desk in surprise.

"Some kind of an accident?" he asked. "I'm Sergeant Marker."

"No," Mr. Hollister replied, "but these children have solved a mystery."

"We've found the stolen coins," Pete said. "They were in the fountain."

"But the coins in the fountain—" the policeman started to say.

"Honest, these are the real stolen ones," Teddy said, and laid the box on the table. Skeptically, the sergeant took a typewritten list from a drawer and began to check the coins against it. After a minute he looked up ruefully.

"What do you know about that? Right under our very noses!"

"Now can Fishy go free?" Pam asked anxiously.

"Perhaps," came the reply. "The chief will have to decide that."

"Please," Jean begged. "Let him go. He's been in jail long enough and we've found the coins."

"He really thought they belonged to him," Pete put in. "Please call the chief now. I'm sure he'll let Fishy go."

Sergeant Marker shook his head doubtfully. "We've never done this before," he said.

"I don't see that it would do any harm," Mr. Hollister remarked.

After several telephone calls the sergeant reported that there would be no charges pressed against Fishy and the chief had instructed him to release the handyman.

When the prisoner was brought from his cell, he came out bleary-eyed and confused.

"I can go home, you say?" he asked the sergeant.

"That's right, we've found the coins. Or rather, the Hollisters have."

The man blinked in astonishment. "How did you know—" he exclaimed.

"That's our secret," Pam replied, smiling. "Maybe someday you'll get the coins that were promised to your father," she said.

Fishy Lucas shook his head in disbelief. He sniffed and wiped his eyes with the back of his hand.

"We'll take you home," Mr. Hollister said. "Our station wagon is right outside."

They all rode silently to the shack where Fishy Lucas lived. When he got out of the car he turned and said, "Thank you, thank you, children," and with his head bent, shuffled off.

"Oh, that poor man," Pam said as they drove on. "I hope he doesn't do anything bad again."

"I doubt that he will," Mr. Hollister replied.

By the time they reached the farm a rim of gray light began to turn pink on the horizon.

"Come now," Mr. Hollister said. "You need some sleep. I'll tell everybody about the mystery as soon as they get up."

"Don't let us sleep too long, Dad," Pete said. "We have a date with Mr. Turner at ten o'clock."

But nobody had to awaken the young detectives. When John Hollister announced to the early risers that the mystery of the lost coins had been solved, they made such a commotion that the four sleepers awoke, jumped out of their beds, dressed hurriedly and came to breakfast, their eyes still squinty from slumber.

Amid the hugs and congratulations, the telephone rang. Holly answered. "It's Oz," she said, and listened while he spoke.

"Oh, that's just dandy!" Holly exclaimed. "Goodby."

She turned to the others. "We were right! It was Joey who called us and pretended to be the thief. He was boasting to Oz how easy it was to fool us. And guess what!" she added happily. "Joey has gone home to Shoreham. Now he won't bother us any more!"

Pete and Teddy could hardly wait for ten o'clock to come. At five minutes to the hour, Pete turned to his cousin and said, "He should arrive any minute. Crickets! If we could solve both mysteries, wouldn't that be great!"

The two boys kept their eyes on the road, but Mr. Turner's car did not appear. At half past ten, Pete started to fidget. "Where can he be?" he asked.

"Maybe he was held up on some kind of business,"

Teddy said. Now the boys walked to the road and looked at every passing car.

By eleven o'clock, Pete said, "Teddy, something's happened. I'm going to call Mr. Turner's office."

He ran inside, dialed the number. The tree man's secretary answered.

"This is Pete Hollister," the boy said. "We're waiting for Mr. Turner to meet us. Is he coming?"

The woman's voice sounded surprised. "Then you changed your mind again?" she asked.

"What do you mean?"

"You phoned Mr. Turner last night and said to forget about helping you. He was very disappointed."

CHAPTER 17

THE GOLF BALL GOOF

PETE was shocked to learn of the fake telephone call to Mr. Turner. "That wasn't I who called," he told the secretary.

"It was a boy and he gave your name," came the reply.

"It must have been Joey Brill," Pete said. "He plays mean tricks like that."

The woman said it was too bad. But on the other hand, Mr. Turner would be glad to hear that Pete had not lost interest in the mystery.

"Where can I get in touch with him now?" Pete asked.

The secretary said that this was Mr. Turner's day off. He had planned to devote it to helping the boys solve the riddle of the treasure oak. Instead, he had gone to play golf, and could be found on the Crestwood Golf Course. Pete thanked the woman and hung up.

"Oh, that Joey!" Pam said when she heard the story. "I'm glad he's gone back home, so he won't bother us."

Pete remembered that the Crestwood Golf Course was on the other side of Bald Eagle Hill. If he could locate Mr. Turner, perhaps they could look for the treasure oak. His mother suggested that first they eat lunch, and after that she would drive them to the golf course.

When they had finished the meal, Sue was left in the charge of Aunt Marge to take an afternoon nap. The other six youngsters climbed into the station wagon and Mrs. Hollister drove toward the golf course.

The road led past Mr. Spencer's estate, took a wide bend around the foot of Bald Eagle Hill, and skirted a long, green fairway. Far in the distance they could see two men approaching a golf tee.

"Maybe one of them is Mr. Turner," Pete said, and asked his mother to stop the car. As she did, one of the golfers hit the ball and it soared high into the air landing with a plop in high grass near the road.

Ricky opened the car door and he and Holly raced toward the ball.

"Come back here," their mother called, but they did not hear her. The two children scampered to where the ball had dropped, and Holly picked it up.

"I suppose the man wants it back," she said.

"If it's Mr. Turner, he'll like our good deed," Ricky said proudly. Together they ran across the fairway, with Holly waving the ball in her right hand.

Seeing what had happened, the golfer waved his arms and shouted something.

"He wants us to hurry," Ricky said. "Come on, let's run faster!"

As the children approached the tee, they could

see that neither man was Mr. Turner. The golfer who had made the shot still held the driver in his hand and strode toward the children. His face was flushed with anger.

"What's the idea!" he cried out. "You shouldn't have touched that ball! That was the longest drive I ever made!"

Ricky and Holly looked up at them, their mouths open in surprise and amazement.

"We—we thought you wanted it back," Ricky managed to say.

"Oh, bosh!" the man declared.

"But it landed in the high grass," Holly said meekly. "Don't you want to try it again?"

When the golfer's partner heard this, he laughed. Holly started to cry. Ricky wanted to run away. He glanced back toward the car to see Pete and Pam hastening across the fairway toward them.

Hot tears ran down Holly's cheeks as she gave the golf ball to the man. Ricky put his arm around her, and said, "Don't cry, Holly."

Now the angry man's face relaxed. He did not want to see a little girl weep.

"All right, I'm sorry I yelled at you," he said. And then his frown was replaced with a smile. "If you thought you were trying to help me, that's fine."

Pete and Pam reached the tee, and they apologized to the man for what had happened. "They really don't know how to play golf," Pam told him. "Come on now," she added, taking Holly's hand.

"I wish I could make up for my rudeness," the golfer said, looking embarrassed.

Holly's eyes brightened at once. "Will you let me hit the ball?"

"Of course. Come over here, I'll show you how." The man pulled a club from his golf bag and placed the ball on a tee. Then he stood behind Holly and put his arms around her, showing how to grasp the club.

When he stepped back, Holly took a big swing. *Whack!* The ball soared into the air and headed straight down the fairway.

"Good for you!" the golfer exclaimed.

"I'm going to be a champion someday," Holly promised, handing back the club.

As Pete turned to leave, he said, "By the way, sir, have you seen Mr. Turner here today?"

"Yes, he went out shortly before we did. You'll probably find him at the clubhouse now." Then he added with a wink, "Please don't tell him that I lost my temper."

"We won't!" Pam said laughing, and the four children returned to the car.

Teddy and Jean were still chuckling about Holly's golf ball adventure when Mrs. Hollister drove up to the clubhouse about a mile away. Pete and Pam went inside and met Mr. Turner who was about to leave.

"I'm sorry you gave up your case," the tree man said.

"Good for you!"

"But we didn't!" Pam explained the hoax to Mr. Turner.

"In that case," the man replied smiling, "I shall be glad to help you."

"Right away?" Pete asked.

"Yes."

"Thank you, Mr. Turner," Pam said and hastened to the car to tell her mother.

"All right," Mrs. Hollister said. "But while you older children are searching for the treasure oak, I want Ricky and Holly to go shopping with me in town. They both need new shoes."

Holly's face fell.

"But Mother," Ricky protested, "we'll miss all the excitement!"

"No you won't," Pete said quickly. "We'll probably have to look at a lot of trees before we find the right one and you can be back by then."

"Daddy or I will bring you here afterward," Mrs. Hollister promised.

Holly brightened. "Will you buy us a chocolate ice cream soda?" she asked. When Mrs. Hollister nodded, the pig-tailed girl gave her a hug.

"We'll all come home with Mr. Turner," Pete said. "Don't worry about us."

Since Bald Eagle Hill was within walking distance, Mr. Turner left his car at the club. Then he and the youngsters hopped the fence, and hiked across the flat meadow of the Spencer estate, until they came to a long slope which led to the top of Bald Eagle Hill.

Pete and Teddy took turns leading the way up through the small trees, which gradually gave way to large oaks and pines. Halfway up the slope they stopped to rest and looked back at the wide, sweeping view behind them. They resumed climbing and after a while Jean said, "I smell smoke."

"Somebody must be having a cookout," Teddy surmised.

"Maybe it's a forest fire," Pam said.

With a worried look, Mr. Turner hurried on ahead. The hill grew steeper and the woods thicker until they reached the top and stood at the edge of the big clearing.

On the other side they could see smoke rising from a bonfire of logs. Beyond it, a husky, bald-headed man was cutting up a fallen pine tree with a power saw. A small truck stood nearby, and as he cut the sections of logs he threw them on the truck.

As they drew closer, the children saw the man approach an uprooted oak tree.

"Crickets!" Pete thought. "Suppose it's the tree we're looking for. When the saw cuts it might destroy the treasure!"

"Mr. Rogers!" he called as he ran forward. "Don't cut that oak tree!"

But the man had already pressed the saw against the trunk and the sound of the motor drowned out Pete's voice. Now everyone, even Mr. Turner, ran with waving arms to attract the man's attention. But his back was turned and he did not see them.

With a burst of speed Pete crossed the clearing. He had almost reached Mr. Rogers when the chain saw bit into the tree bark, scattering chips in all directions.

"I've got to stop him!" the boy said to himself.

In his excitement Pete did not notice a yawning pit left by the uprooted oak tree. He pitched into the hole and blacked out!

CHAPTER 18

THE OAK TREE'S SECRET

TEDDY and Jean raced past, calling for Mr. Rogers not to cut the oak tree. Hearing them, the caretaker stopped in surprise, laid his saw down and shut off the motor.

Pam and Mr. Turner, meanwhile, went to Pete's aid. His sister hopped down into the hole, where the boy lay still. "Pete!" she cried, shaking his shoulder.

"He's been knocked out," Mr. Turner said. He and Pam lifted the boy out of the hole and laid him on the ground, as the caretaker, Teddy and Jean hurried over. Pete's face was pale, and a large bump stood out on his forehead. Pam chafed her brother's wrists while the tree man loosened the boy's shirt.

Pete's eyes flickered open and he said in a weak voice, "Did-did he cut the tree?"

"Just about an inch," Mr. Rogers said. "Don't worry, son."

Pete shook his head, as if to clear the cobwebs from his brain. "I'm all right now," he said sheepishly and rose to his feet. "I should have looked where I was going."

When his companions were sure that Pete had recovered, they told the caretaker about their search for the mystery oak.

"The one we're looking for," Mr. Turner said, "will have a scar on the trunk."

"It will also probably look like the oak tree on this coin," Pete added, and pulled the shilling from his pocket.

With a wave of his hand Mr. Rogers said, "There are a lot of oaks to choose from. Take your pick."

The searchers went from oak tree to oak tree, looking for scars which might indicate a wound made long ago in the bark. After an hour's tramp around the crown of the hill, Mr. Turner and the children had picked out thirteen likely trees, including the one which the caretaker had begun to cut.

"Which looks most like the tree on the shilling?" Pam asked as they stopped in the shade of leafy branches and gazed around the hilltop.

"That's hard to tell with so much foliage," Mr. Turner said.

Pete cocked his head sideways and took a long look at a tree which had been tilted by the tornado. "That might be it," he said. "Do you suppose we could trim off some of the leaves to get a better look?"

Mr. Turner said this could be done, provided they had a saw.

"I have a couple in my truck. You can use them," the caretaker said, "but how're you going to climb up there?" Doubtfully, he eyed the lowest branch which was far above their reach.

"We'll make a human ladder," the boy replied, "if you'll help us."

"Well, that's an idea!" The big man chuckled. "I guess you want me for the bottom."

"That's right," said Pete.

Quickly the girls ran to the truck and brought back two saws. While Mr. Rogers crouched at the foot of the tree, Teddy climbed to his broad shoulders, steadying himself against the rough tree trunk. Then Mr. Turner bent over and from his back Pete climbed to Teddy's shoulders, and swung himself up onto a branch.

The girls handed the saws up to Teddy, and he passed them to Pete who then helped his cousin clamber into the tree. Working their way from limb to limb the boys sawed off the smaller branches with the most leaves. As the foliage swished to the ground the outline of the old, crippled oak became plainer.

"That's fine!" Mr. Turner cried. "You've done enough now—come on down." With the help of the two men the boys eased themselves to the ground. Then as Pam held the coin, they compared the Oak Tree shilling with the tree before them.

"Look here," Mr. Turner said, as he traced his finger along the coin. "The conformation is just about the same."

"I think this is our tree!" Pete exclaimed.

"That's lucky," the caretaker said, "because this one has to come down anyway. The storm damaged it pretty badly."

"But there are so many scars on the trunk," Jean said. "How do we know which one marks the treasure?"

Mr. Turner advised that the tree be cut up into small logs, taking care not to saw through the scars. "Then we can take the sections back to Mr. Spencer's estate and split them," the tree man said.

"Crickets!" Pete exclaimed. "Let's start right away, Mr. Rogers."

"Stand back, then," the caretaker replied. "Here we go!"

While the others watched, the husky man felled the oak tree. Then he and Mr. Turner carefully cut the trunk into small lengths. There were scars on seven of the logs. These the cousins carefully loaded onto the truck.

"The best way to split these logs open," Mr. Rogers commented as they drove along the bumpy road, "is with a sledge hammer and wedges."

"Daddy has some at home," Jean said. "He's very good at splitting logs."

The truck stopped beside an old well behind Mr. Spencer's house. Nearby there were neat stacks of firewood. "This is where I usually chop wood," said the caretaker. Pete and Teddy threw the logs to the ground, while Pam went inside the house to telephone for Uncle Russ. When she came out, Mr. Spencer was with her, just as excited as the children. A few minutes later Pam's father and Uncle Russ arrived with the tools necessary to split the big oak logs. They brought Ricky and Holly with them.

Everyone gathered around as Mr. Hollister and his brother made ready to crack open the wood. "Stay back, now," Uncle Russ warned.

"Oh, I *do* hope we find the treasure!" Pam said breathlessly.

Mr. Hollister held the wedge against the flat surface of the log while Uncle Russ tapped it into place. Then, with mighty swings, the cartoonist wielded the sledge hammer. The iron head crashed down against the wedge, making the split in the log grow wider and wider. Finally, with a ringing *clang!* the log separated. The children rushed forward. Nothing was in it.

"Let's try the next one, John," Uncle Russ said.

Another log was put in place and the wedge driven in.

Bang—Bang—Bang! The log fell apart. The children were disappointed again. No treasure.

"Here try this one," Mr. Turner suggested, as he rolled the third log into place. Pete noticed that it had an extra large scar on its side resembling a gnarled fist.

"Let me take a whack at this one," Mr. Hollister said.

"Okay, John."

When the wedge had been put in place, Mr. Hollister raised the hammer high over his head and brought it down with a crash. The wedge zipped through the log, which fell in half as if it had been a peanut.

"Oh look!" Holly shouted. "Something's in it!"

"Yikes!" Ricky yelped.

A shiny metal surface about as big as a silver dollar shone through one of the split surfaces of the log.

"It looks like the end of a pipe," Mr. Hollister said, picking up the wedge. "Hold the other half of the log for me, Russ. I'll split it again."

"The treasure! We found the treasure!" Jean cried, clapping her hands.

"Stand back, everybody," Mr. Hollister ordered.

The first blow put a crack in the log and the man poised himself for another stroke with the hammer. Down it came. *Wham!*

The wood cracked open. And as it did, a metal object sailed over the heads of the children. It banged against the little roof over the well, then disappeared down the big black hole.

"It's-it's gone! We've lost it!" Holly wailed as the cousins raced over to look down the well.

"It must have been the treasure!" Pete exclaimed.

"And how will we get it?" Teddy asked.

The caretaker quickly ran for a ladder, but he could not put it down into the well because of the roof built over it.

"Yikes!" Ricky said. "I have an idea. Why don't I ride down in the bucket?"

The grownups looked at one another skeptically.

"Sure, he's small enough to fit in," Pete said. "Let him try, Dad."

"The well is dry," Mr. Spencer reminded them.

"And the bucket and chain are sound," Mr. Rogers put in.

"I think your boy would be safe," Mr. Spencer assured them.

"He has my vote," Mr. Turner said with a wide grin.

"All right," Mr. Hollister agreed. "Come on, Ricky, into the bucket."

The boy sat inside the old wooden tub and clung to the chain with both hands. His father and the tree man turned the crank slowly, lowering the pail deep down into the old well.

"Are you all right?" Pam called down.

Ricky's voice floated up hollowly. "Okay, I'm near the bottom."

Suddenly there was a sharp cry. "I've got it! I've got it, Dad! Pull me up!"

The bucket came up slowly as the iron chain creaked with every turn of the windlass. "Oh hurry, Daddy, hurry!" Holly begged. Finally Ricky's red head emerged and eager hands swung him safely out of the well.

"Look, I got it!" Ricky cried, holding up a section of pipe. It was about eight inches long and capped at either end. He handed it to Mr. Spencer.

"So this is the treasure," the man said. "I wonder

The men lowered Ricky into the dry well.

what my father had in mind when he planted it in the tree many years ago."

"We'll need a couple of wrenches to open the tube," Mr. Hollister told him.

"You'll find them in my workshop," Mr. Spencer said, turning to his caretaker. "Go fetch them, would you?"

Mr. Rogers hurried off and returned with two large wrenches. Mr. Hollister took them. Expertly he grasped the pipe in the jaws of one wrench. With the second, he gripped one of the caps, then, straining with all his might, carefully put pressure on the threads.

Slowly the cap turned.

"Crickets, Daddy, you did it!" Pete said as Mr. Hollister quickly unscrewed the one end.

When the cap came off Mr. Hollister tilted the pipe on the ground. Out poured several dozen old coins.

The children shouted and clapped, and the grown-ups exclaimed in amazement.

"You've done it again, children!" Mr. Hollister said proudly. "You've solved the secret of the coins."

Pete was kneeling on the ground with the other children and Mr. Spencer, examining the old pieces. "Dad, they're lucky coins!" the boy exclaimed.

"What do you mean?" Ricky asked.

"Lucky for Fishy Lucas," Pete replied. "These are the ones that old Mr. Spencer promised to give Fishy Lucas's father."

"He's not the only one who's fortunate," Mr. Spencer said with a smile. "There are other fine coins here too, including a Flying Eagle cent."

Pete gave a little whistle as Mr. Spencer let him look at it. "1858," the boy said. "We read about it in our catalogue."

"The Flying Eagle is very valuable," Pam added.

Pete returned the cent to its owner, and helped him scoop all the other coins into his hand. "This is fantastic," the man said as he rose to his feet. "I've never heard of anything like it before." Then a twinkle shone in his eyes and he added, "Will you all meet me at the museum in an hour?"

"We sure will!" Pete said.

"Do you have a surprise?" Holly asked.

"I don't think there is any surprise bigger than the one you children have just given me. But I have something in mind. See you later."

The Hollisters took Mr. Turner back to his car, then returned to the farm to tell the startling news of the discovery in the old oak tree.

An hour later all the Hollisters arrived at the Crestwood town square and walked into the museum. Ricky took a backward, longing look at the fountain with its spray sparkling in the sunlight, but Pam tugged his hand and they all marched inside.

Mr. Spencer was already there with Sergeant Costello and Fishy Lucas. Everyone was ushered into the room where the old coins had been on exhibit. The collection was back under glass in a new velvet-lined box, and on top of the display case were spread the coins which the children had found in the oak tree.

When they had all gathered around the exhibit, Mr. Spencer spoke up. "This is a happy day for me," he said. "The Hollisters have solved *three* mysteries, really."

He praised them for their detective work in locating the missing coin collection. "Then they found the old deed," the man added, "and now they've discovered the treasure in the oak tree."

"It was fun doing it," Holly piped up.

Pete grinned. "It made a swell vacation for us."

"You were a big help to the police department," the sergeant put in. "And I'm sure Fishy is grateful to you because you spoke up for him."

"Furthermore," Mr. Spencer said. "Fishy is going to work for me from now on. Mr. Rogers needs an assistant."

"Oh goody!" Sue said and clapped her chubby hands. Murmurs of approval were heard from the grownups.

Mr. Spencer then motioned toward the coins lying on top of the glass. "The ones promised to old Mr. Lucas will go to Fishy," he said. "The rest I will put in my father's collection—all except one." He reached over and picked up the Flying Eagle cent. "This is for the Shoreham Hollisters to add to their penny collection."

"Yikes!" Ricky cried. "That's the one that's worth four hundred dollars!"

"Crickets!" Pete said. "We're rich!"

Laughter and handshaking followed, but Fishy Lucas had tears in his eyes.

"Thank you, thank you," was all he could say to the children.

Holly and Ricky grabbed his hands and tugged him toward the door. "Where are you taking me?" Fishy asked.

"To the fountain," Holly replied and pulled a penny from her pocket. "We're going to wish you good luck from now on!"